CHRISTMAS
AT
GREEN RIVER COVE

*If you could go
home again,
would you?*

D1004273

LISA COLODNY

Copyright

Editing by Pure Grammar Editorial Services
- www.puregrammar.com
Formatting & Cover Design by KP Designs
- www.kpdesignshop.com
Published by Kingston Publishing Company
- www.kingstonpublishing.com

Table of Contents

Chapter 1

It was interesting how quickly the scenery changed as a journey moved from the massiveness of the interstate to the first of many quaint country roads, especially if the road bent and twisted to such extent. It felt as if she should have offered a ticket to a carnival attendant before buckling the seat belt. Avery gripped the steering wheel tighter and adjusted herself more comfortably in the driver's seat, as if she were navigating an airplane onto a runway instead of keeping the car centered perfectly on one side of the two-lane road. It was a skill she knew she possessed or had once upon a time when she was younger. No doubt, it would be like riding a bike once she reacquainted herself with the terrain.

The route was familiar, at least it had been once, many years ago. It was scary how quickly time got away. One minute, you were seventeen years old and accessing potential colleges to suit your specific career path. The next minute, you're performing the same task for your daughter and hoping your ex-husband is still amenable to splitting the expenses, given how she opted for an out-of-state college instead of the one in North Carolina where her college was already prepaid. That was a discussion for another time as her immediate task was to focus on the road and ensure there was not an accidental engagement of "ding dong mailbox." Had the mailboxes always been so snug to the road? She did not recollect it as such.

The scenery, too, was a distraction as she fought the urge to look away from the road and admire the scattered farmhouses as they prepared for the long, cold winter ahead. Spring and summer in Kentucky were beautiful as evidenced by the State's focus during the televised running of the Derby. But the Fall foliage was also a sight to behold with its rainbow of gold and red bursting from the tree line like soldiers holding a line. It took her breath away; she could not remember seeing it more beautiful.

Fall was evident everywhere she looked, as far she could see, there was not a speck of green. Still, it had a beauty of its own as the branches of some trees jutted out, naked, barren of a leaf of any type. While another, not thirty feet away, was alive with yellow, brown, and red leaves—its shape a bouquet of color.

And the fields, who just a few short months ago, were blanketed with luscious green stalks of corn and bushes of soybean, lay barren with only skeletonized, dead stalks that had escaped from the picker while the corn was harvested or cut. From a distance, drying stalks of tobacco were visible through the open door of a massive red barn that faced the roadway. She thought immediately of days long past when she was young and rode the tobacco setter with her cousin. Although the trip home was primarily one centered around business, it would be good to reconnect with her family and friends as it had been many years since she had been in Green River Cove for anything other than a funeral or wedding.

Three weeks, she exhaled a breath, allowing the realization to sink in and allowing time for the knot in her throat to dissipate. It would take about three weeks to finalize the acquisition of the town's local bottling company by her current employer, Leopold Media. It was all but a done deal, Cove Bottling, who had enjoyed a long history spanning multiple generations of producing and locally distributing several brands of soda, was to be purchased by Leopold Media. Once acquired, the Cove facility would enjoy multiple factory upgrades and have the vast resources of Leopold Media to expand its distribution well past the central Kentucky counties where it was currently available.

It was an exciting time for Green River Cove whose most popular soda, Rush, would be available on a more National market as well as be a reprieve for its owner, Patterson Milby, whose struggle to keep the company viable was not a secret. It was a win, win for everyone involved, including Avery, and she could not wait to arrive in Green River Cove and get started.

****

When her car rolled past the sign that read Hardyville, she knew the road would connect directly to Highway 88. The words rolled off her tongue as if she were greeting an old friend, one she expected to run into, but the remnants of the encounter were like an aftershock of a much larger event. Her grandfather's country store and the roller-skating rink were both stretched out along the highway as if they were breadcrumbs leading the way home. Each leaning mailbox and dirt road, a testament that the distance was growing smaller.

She hit the brake as her car sped past an old boarded-up wooden building with faded and peeling white paint only visible in a few scarce places. The rusty, metal awning, supported by only a single bracket, hung sideways atop the boarded-over front door. There was a large area of brown, dead grass in what would have been the parking area and a line of tall weeds grew from the wide spaces where planks of wood were missing from the porch. Painted upon the wall, in a place just about the height of a vending machine, the word, Rush, was barely recognizable.

Avery did not need to exhaust any energy in deciphering the rest of faded green, letters. She knew what message it had once delivered. Once upon a time, her steady hand had painted the mural upon the wall at her grandfather's request. It had read, Life's a Rush. Get yours here! She smiled, thinking how true the words had been back then. And hoped to recapture just a fraction of that feeling during her trip home.

She was barely able to make out the outline of the old skating rink as her car grew closer to its image behind the thick trunks of black trees. Although most of the trees were naked of any leaves, the limbs that bordered the property were thick and mangled one into the other, looking like something out of a Grimm's fairytale. The building, itself, had fallen upon hard times with most of its roof missing, and what was left of its skeletonized frame, hanging broken and bent. It was obvious no one had been inside in a long time and her heart ached at the thought. Many a Friday night had been spent inside the old place, with music belching out into the field behind the rink and across the open spaces between the closest farms. How many nights had she waited outside for her ride, swaying to the music from within with her best friends at her side and hoping the couples dance might have been enough of a hint to prompt Aidan into asking her to middle school homecoming?

Her smile was still evident as she entered the city limits and let the car idle down so that she could be compliant with the speed limit. She was certain Sheriff Newton had long since retired but she had heard a rumor his son had taken over the responsibility. Evan, probably, would not have given her a ticket but best not to tempt fate. High school was over long ago, and like the skating rink, things had changed.

****

Once she turned the car onto Main Street, she slowed down literally to a snail's pace, mostly to avoid colliding with the beat-up old, delivery truck from Minor's Market as it crawled its way from the corner drug store to the end of the street where the café was located. The aged driver, Mr. Minor edged his truck to the right, practically pulling atop the curb, leaving just enough space for the traffic behind him to pass. Avery checked the mirror, ensuring there was enough space between his truck and her to car to safely pass when he called out from the open window, "Welcome home!"

"Thank you," she waved back, hoping the driver behind her realized the forward motion of her own car had ceased, and she could respond to him through the open passenger window.

"How long you home for?" he asked as the truck belched and coughed while he slid the gear shift into park and pushed the driver's door open in the same motion.

"However long it takes for the merger," she paused, hoping her response had not sounded as if she was in a hurry to return to North Carolina because she was not. The time she planned to be in Green River Cove was going to be a welcomed change. "About three weeks," she added quickly.

"I know Ward and Patricia will be glad to have you home for such a long spell." He slid his bulky body out of the truck's cab, adjusting the loosely hanging strap of his Duck Head overalls tight atop his shoulder. "Business at the bookstore has been slow. It was the perfect time for some renovations there and at your old house."

"Mom mentioned to me, they were having the kitchen remodeled and pulling up the old carpet." She waved, "I'll see soon, Mr. Minor."

He slammed the door, smiling as she pulled her car away. "Wait till you see what they did at the shop with your book."

Her book? She glanced at his retreating figure in the rearview mirror as if he could read her mind and repeat whatever he had said about her book. She knew without checking in the mirror, her face was flushed, crimson red as deep a color as the poinsettias that lined the window box like statues in the glass window of the flower shop.

Writing that book had been her accomplishment of many years ago, she rationalized. She was fresh out of high school and registered for as many college classes she believed would help her dream of becoming a writer, be a reality.

Luckily, she had the good sense to complete a dual curriculum, one that included business. So that when writing had not panned out, she had been able to find dutiful employment with a business degree. No one at Leopold Media even knew about her bestselling debut novel—and with continued luck, they would never find out. She was a one-hit wonder as her second book did not even make it off her publisher's desk. Her writing career was news only to those who lived in or around Green River Cove and Avery was perfectly fine with the limited notoriety.

****

The bell that hung over the door at the bookstore to announce the arrival of a customer was just as annoying as she remembered, maybe more so. Time away had done little to improve her patience. She took a moment to assess the bookstore, noting that although many of the books were different, the general make-up of the store was not. To her immediate right, was the same old gold sofa and wooden coffee table she remembered, even the black, wrought iron lamps were the same. It was a cozy reading area with enough space to enjoy a coffee and peruse the book a final time before opting to make the purchase.

Behind the couch, were rows and rows of heavily ladened shelves, bursting with enough books to the extent some were stacked cover to cover across the top of the shelf as if waiting for an empty space somewhere within the shelf. Both windows had frilly white lace curtains tethered back against the walls so that there was full visibility out of the windows and into the quaint storefront of Main Street. Near the back, an old register marked the top of a worn, old cabinet being used as a counter. There was barely enough space for a sole person and only one wicker chair to accommodate whoever was minding the register.

"Ward! She's here!" her mother's voice echoed from the back of the store before she stepped into view from behind one of the shelves.

"Mom," Avery smiled, rushing into her mom's embrace as if she had not seen her in years, even though both her parents had attended their granddaughter, Samantha's, high school graduation just a few months prior. Patricia was an attractive woman, especially for her age. It seemed most thought her to be twenty years younger than she was. Something she never grew tired of hearing. As such, she paid careful attention to her hair and makeup and she was among Green River Cove's most fashionable, yet conservative dressers.

Ward was the perfect complement to his wife's outgoing personality. Like her, he was warm and friendly, but with a penance to be more reserved and in thoughtful conversation with himself. His smile was infectious, so that it started at his lips but ran up the length of his cheeks and ended at the tip of a cow's lick in the center of his forehead, with just enough force so that his hazel eyes all but disappeared between the folds of skin. He loved to tell a good joke and his laughter would sometimes echo from the bookshop all the way to the end of the street where Paige's Bakery was located.

"Was beginning to think Mr. Leopold changed his mind and you were waiting to deliver bad news." Her mother pulled away from the embrace and took a moment to study her daughter before adding. "You've lost more weight?" Although it was meant as a question, it did not come out that way and Avery knew that responding either way would surely lead to a more through discussion around the topic of her divorce and long work hours.

It was better to just avoid both topics and respond to her mother's initial concern. "No, Matthew Leopold is not the type of man who changes his mind, although he has been known to change his approach." She met her father in the space behind the couch and leaned into his embrace. "Store looks great, Dad."

"Welcome home, Baby," he pulled her by the arm towards the last bookcase where a sign with a picture of the state of Kentucky was posted at the top of the first shelf. Printed in small block letters within the state was the word, *Authors*. He laughed and pushed his hand through his thick, white hair. "You're in good company." He traced his finger along the spine of several books by authors like Wendell Berry, Janice Holt Giles, Edgar Cayce, Harry Caudill, and others before he tapped one with her name on its cover. There was only one copy of her novel, *Sanctuary Road,* lined with the others but he had several other copies stacked cover to cover on the bottom shelf.

"Dad," she smiled, but felt the embarrassment rise like steam to the surface of her skin. "You are probably the only store in the Eastern part of the country to carry my book. It's been out of print for years."

"It's still available for print on demand," his chest heaved proudly, "but every town your mother and I visit, we check out the bookstores to see if any copies are available." He tapped the bottom shelf with the tip of his foot. "I hit the motherload in a bargain bookseller in E town last month."

His words seemed far away as her attention fell upon a set of three books bound together and displayed atop an antique desk and lantern. "I can't believe you held onto these." She approached the desk as if it were an old friend and gathered the books in her hand.

"My favorite book by that author," he smiled and moved as close to her as he could, pulling one of the books from the binding and holding it out to her. "You should have at least kept one copy."

"There was no point once the publisher returned it to me. I could only afford to print four copies," she laughed, sliding the book back between the cloth binding that held the others. "And you're missing one copy, Dad."

"That's okay, it'll show up," he pulled her into his arms momentarily for another hug before stepping away and looking upon her as if she were an apparition. "And I don't care what the publisher said, Honey, these stories were amazing. You should have tried another publisher who managed different genres than that of your first novel."

"My life as a writer was over before it even started," she pulled her bag as high atop her shoulder as she could. "I wrote a hot, steamy romance novel that I loathed, and it became a best seller while my collection of heartwarming, socially appropriate short stories was returned with barely a page turned. I'd be surprised if they reviewed any more than the first two stories before returning it to me."

She reached for the door, "Was a long time ago, Dad. I'm happier on this career path than I would have been as a writer. There were just too many variables, too many things that couldn't be controlled." Avery leaned in and kissed his cheek. "I'll see you back at the house?"

"Yes," he shook his head, letting his hand with her books drop to his side. "Dinner in town, later?"

"Sure," she blew a kiss to her mother. "Key still under the ceramic planter?" She did not need to wait for either of them to respond. She knew the key would be there, waiting for her or one of her siblings to need it. It was known, a commonality of life in Green River Cove; one that like the thought of her grandfather's store or the skating rink was comforting.

****

Her old room at her parents' house had not changed much in the years since she had left for college.

It was as if her parents assumed she might return one day and find a use for the track trophies that lined the shelves, posters that covered the walls, and stuffed animals that occupied the center of her bed. Even her desk was as she had left it, its top barely visible under the typewriter and stacks of composition books. From her earliest recollections she had used composition books to secure her most treasured thoughts and memories. And they were all there as she had left them, stacked alphabetically from A to Z to represent the working titles she had given her essays.

Randomly, she selected one of the books and leafed through its pages, watching as the words flew by as if fast forwarding through the scenes of a movie. She paused for a minute to reflect upon a story she had penned as First Love and saw the night's events in her mind as if reliving prom night all over again. It had been a magical night, perfect in almost every way, except the night had been their first and last date and she never really knew why.

Avery did not realize how tired she was until she gathered her senior yearbook from the shelf and fell atop the bed, careful to disrupt her stuffed furry friends as little as possible. Her eyes grew heavy as she turned the pages, smiling at the youthful reflection of herself looking back from the slick, shiny pages as she posed alongside her friends for various clubs and teams.

There was Paige and Brooke, her best friends since elementary school, who stood at her side through middle and high school. They were the three musketeers in everything they did. She sighed, aside from birthday cards every April and June, she had not had much engagement with either of them. And since both still lived in Green River Cove, that was sure to change over the next three weeks.

Paige was the unofficial leader of the trio, the first to suggest what opportunities the night might hold for them or what movie was possibly the most appropriate. She was outspoken to a fault and the one most likely to recall the name of anyone she had ever met. In school, she had worn her long blonde hair, straight, hanging low past her shoulders. Now that she was older, she wore it curlier and shorter so that it just kissed the top pf her shoulders. She married her high school sweetheart, Griffin, right after graduation and started a family soon after with the arrival of a daughter, Nancy, and son Ian.

Griffin was one of Green River Cove's most successful general contractors whose expertise and skill were evident on many structures throughout the town. In his free time, he enjoyed playing bluegrass music with a small group of friends. They performed frequently at various local functions in and around town. Like her father, Nancy had both a knack for music and business and was following in her father's footsteps with the same precision and confidence as her mother.

Her son, Ian, was less interested in his father's business. Instead, he passed his free time drawing and sketching anything of interest in and around the town he loved with all his heart. His first unofficial paid assignment had been to design the posters and graphics for his mother's campaign as mayor of Green River Cove. It was no surprise to anyone that knew Paige when she won the office, she was one of the most well-respected and likable citizens in the community and would do only good things for the town.

Brooke's hair was darker and thicker, looking as if she had undergone a continuous permanent that left it curly, especially at the ends. Her eyes were amazing crystal blue — so light they looked almost white against the rising sun. She was tall and leaner than either Paige or Avery, and she was the first of the trio to require a training bra. As a result, Brooke became the unofficial confidant of all things related to growing up, including but not limited to dating, kissing, or sex.

Like Paige, Brooke married her high school sweetheart, Graham, a drummer in the high school marching band. He was thick and tall, built like a mountain with the most gorgeous curly blonde hair and blue eyes, she had ever seen. Brooke left Green River Cove only long enough to attend and finish law school while Graham finished nursing school. The fruits of their life together produced two sons, Stephen, who was currently enrolled as a cadet in the police academy while the younger son, Patrick, was only weeks away from completing basic training as a soldier in the U.S. Army.

Their life in Green River Cove was complete as Brooke's law practice flourished and Graham worked his way into an administrative nursing position at the local hospital. They wanted nothing more than to celebrate the upcoming holiday with both sons in attendance, but that seemed unlikely as Patrick was not granted leave. It would be her first Christmas without both of her sons and Brooke was miserable at the thought.

Avery yawned into her hand and flipped the page of the yearbook, resting her eyes upon familiar faces, many of whom she had not seen since graduation night. She had not dallied long in Green River Cove once graduation was over, opting instead for early admission into University of Kentucky's liberal arts program where she could only imagine the literary life that awaited her. Her first novel, Sanctuary Road, had undergone significant editorial changes from the publisher before it finally made it to the market. Hotter, she heard repeatedly, and steamier. It was a theme that haunted her every time she met with the editor. If Avery wanted the book to be published, she had to make revisions and produce the story the publisher wanted to be told. It was not necessarily the story Avery wanted to tell but her desire to be published was greater. Quicker than the time it took to sign her name on the contract, she had sacrificed her principles and wrote the story they wanted instead of the one she wanted to tell.

By the time, she met her future husband, Craig, she had already changed her major and was only a few credits shy of a business degree. Their married life together was good, until it wasn't. By then, they both had successful careers with big bank accounts and a baby on the way. For a while, life was good again and then it wasn't, again. The divorce had been little more than an exercise, a meeting with a judge who waved a magic wand and advised that the marriage was done, over. It was as if it never existed at all, and she might have believed that if not for the daughter she loved with all her heart.

Samantha was perfect, the best parts of each of them. Her hair was dark and thick, as were her eyes, like her fathers. She had her mother's smile and laugh and a flair for penning stories and poems at the drop of a hat. At eighteen, she knew everything about everything, including how she did not want to attend a college in North Carolina. She had to go to the University of Kentucky, or her world would surely end, sooner instead of later. Avery was secretly pleased when the decision was made to send her to University of Kentucky for her freshmen year. And Avery's heart had skipped a beat when Samantha left for college wearing wildcat blue.

By the time Avery flipped to the section in the book that contained the class pictures, the sun was setting and the room had darkened to such extent, she reached across the bed and flipped on the lamp. It was as if she was seeing her old habitat for the first time again, and she felt the chill of the encounter as if she had just walked into the room.

The chill, she reiterated, was from being back home in her old room. It had nothing to do with the young innocent face of her prom date staring back at her from the page of the yearbook. Rhem was in the same grade as she had been. In fact, they had spent the entire year before the end of the year getting to know one another in History class and flipping folded sheets of paper that resembled a football across the desks into one another's U-shaped hands in imitation of a field goal.

Sixth period had become her favorite class, all because of the way he flirted and teased her for the entire fifty-five minutes of the class. And when he asked her to attend their senior prom with him, it was by far her most celebrated moment of her entire high school life. Almost immediately, the planning began. What color they would wear, what kind of corsage she wanted, and what type of flower he wanted for his boutonniere?

By the time May rolled around, prom was all she thought about and the hours ticked away like months before it had finally arrived. They had danced every dance, even the fast ones, and the night had been something out of fairytale—except after he dropped her off, they had never interacted in any capacity after that. And to this day, she did not know why.

Chapter 2

Someone, probably her Mom, had turned her bedroom light off during the night. This act only added to her confusion upon awakening in the familiar yet less familiar surroundings of her room. It took mere seconds for her mind to register where she was and her purpose for being there. The closed yearbook lay forgotten on the floor, pushed nearly under the bed, among plastic bins of winter clothes and bathing suits.

It had been many years since she had even thought about Rhem or her senior prom and there was little benefit of doing so now. Last she heard, he had married someone from Anderson County and was coaching high school basketball there. The chance of even running into him over the next three weeks was improbable at best. There was nothing to be concerned or anxious about. She no longer harbored any feelings, good or bad, about him. He was like her grandfather's old store and the skating rink—part of her past.

One thing she was curious about was the amount of renovation going on at her parents' house. The entire house, inside and outside, had been painted with warm colors inside and bolder colors on the trim outside as if to emphasize the unique features of the old farmhouse. The inside was noticeably absent of larger bulkier pieces of furniture as if her mother wanted to give the appearance that the rooms were larger than they were. And the stained scaffolding that hovered over the back wall like judge and jury, only augmented the perception that the room had been staged as if preparing for a performance.

Griffin's construction company had successfully transitioned the wooden front porch into a peaceful and tranquil environment with white-washed walls and distressed garden benches and tables. Swatches of material draped over the back of the bench provided the only source of color against the rising sun. No doubt, renovations would soon begin on the deck in the backyard as well, as evidenced by stacks of plywood piled nearby. Towards the back of the yard, against the aged wooden fence, dozens of trees with burlap-wrapped root balls lay on their side as if they were resting. Pallets of smaller plants and bushes were lined from the back of the house around to the side, stopping just near the front porch where smaller, thinner bushes had been marked for removal. No doubt, the house would have an eye-stopping curb appeal by Spring. If

Avery did not know better, she might think they were planning on selling the place, but that was preposterous. Where else would they go? They had lived all their lives in Green River Cove. Where else would they go?

****

Perspective is something that is unique to the beholder, akin to one's personality or preference to like or dislike a specific food or fragrance. As Avery walked the short walk from the bookstore to Paige's Bakery, her mind spun at the implications at how different the town looked.

True, the businesses were the same, located in the exact places they had been when Avery was younger and living among the Green River Cove community. But for as familiar as they were, they were not the same either. It was like being in awe of Grandma's massive red cookie jar with the big yellow flowers. And how, as a child, both arms were required to pull it across the counter, close enough to reach inside where its sugary treats were contained. Only to encounter it again as an adult and be taken aback by how small it is. As a child, the town felt bigger and she was bewildered at how compact, yet bijou it was.

Paige had changed very little over the years; her laugh and mannerisms were the same as when they had been in school. Yet, there was maturity and self-satisfaction that Avery could only surmise came through Paige's evolution into the woman she is now. Her smile was genuine as she pushed herself into the booth Avery already occupied and slid a saucer with a chocolate drizzled croissant across the table, watching as it came to a stop directly under Avery's chin.

"I remember how much you liked those," she laughed and refilled Avery's cup before pouring two fresh ones and pushing one near the empty place next to Avery. "Brooke should be along, although she runs about ten minutes late to everything." Her laugh was loud and boisterous as it echoed across the room, not bothered by the many heads that spun around in inquiry.

"You've done a good job with the old bakery," Avery fashioned another glance around the dining area, taking note of the many upgrades that had transitioned the old bakery. It had gone from simply being a few metal tables with red speckled Formica tops stationed in front of a tall, heavy pick-up counter to the elegant dining area whose many tables bled charm and character. The bistro tables were either white or black with coordinating iron chairs in a contradictory color to the table.

Each table was adorned with seasonal centerpieces, no doubt compliments of Annetta's, a local flower shop nearby. Along the walls, there were paintings and sketches of familiar local attractions like the old courthouse located in the center of Main Street or the Montgomery mansion where dozens of confederate soldiers were offered sanctuary during the civil war. Atop the buffets and displayed on various shelves were wooden bowls and plates carved from full size tree trunks by a local artisan, Roger Watson, who lived on the other side of the footbridge between town and the elementary school. His pieces were both contemporary and classical, concurrently, depending upon the eye of the beholder, emphasizing again, how important perspective can be. It can be as simple as assessing the girth of a cookie jar or the reasoning behind a rejection.

"Sorry, I'm late," Brooke called from the door as soon as she crossed the threshold into the dining area. "Your office requested some additional documents from Cove, and I wanted to see that they got everything they needed."

"What kind of documents?" Avery asked, surprised she had not been included in the request. It was, after all, her project to manage.

"Additional tax documents for another five years," Brooke pulled a big portion from Avery's pastry and pushed it into her mouth, her eyes rolling for additive effect. "I swear, Paige. No one makes these like you do." She pushed the remnant back towards Avery. "Do croissants in North Carolina taste like these?"

"No," Avery answered, her words distracted as she made no attempt to disguise her concern. "I provided ten years of past returns in the closing documents as was requested?"

"I know but Leopold's assistant called and asked for more, going back at least another five years. It was no problem providing them." She finished off the last of the dessert and wrapped her hand around the coffee cup. "Patterson Milby is anxious to close the deal." She stole a glance behind her and lowered her voice so that the discussion could not be overheard. "He's been struggling these last few years to keep the plant afloat. It's no secret, he's considered selling at least twice before but couldn't find just the right company to sell Cove to."

She was right, Patterson Milby was the fourth generation of Milbys who owned and managed the bottling plant. Children, going back as early as 1956, had enjoyed the citrus flavor of Rush soda with its unique combination of orange and lemon juices. As well, Avery and her elementary classmates had enjoyed the annual end-of-school-year visit from the Rush locomotive who traveled to the school yard at recess with the musical arrangement of the Entertainer bellowing from inside. Once parked, the school children would line up and tour through the train, exiting with a glass bottle of Rush soda, a bag of chips, and a green Rush pencil. It was one of Avery's fondest memories and one of the reasons she transported cases of Rush back to North Carolina every chance she got.

"I'm glad Patterson thinks your company is the right partner. I'd hate to think of the many changes that will occur once the acquisition is completed," Paige added, motioning to one of the servers that she and her guests needed coffee refills.

"Matthew Leopold was impressed with Cove and with the Milby family. Part of the agreement is that the existing leadership team stays in place for one year after the acquisition to ensure a smooth transition of ownership," Avery added. "He has cases of Rush in his office. I think he's a fan too."

"Good," Brooke waited for her cup to be topped off. "Did you get my text about volunteering for the Silent Night Celebration this year since you're going to be here?"

"Thanksgiving was just last week," Avery rubbed her forehead, feigning an ache. "Is it time for that already?"

"We've been having planning meetings for months," Paige answered before Brooke could. "Hoped the old hotel renovation would be farther along but there have been so many issues with permitting and inspections, I bet Rhem is sorry he even had the thought."

"Rhem?" Avery tried to hide her interest, although she was not sure why. These were her oldest and dearest friends; they would know as soon as she repeated his name she was wondering when he had returned to Green River Cove.

"He bought the old hotel on Main Street," Brooke added, "hoping to be able to save it instead of demolishing it like the city council advised."

"I thought he'd left Green River Cove?" the question fought to slide past her lips. Why hadn't her parents told her he had returned?

"He did, but came home after his momma passed," Paige exchanged a quick glance with Brooke. "He's been divorced a year or so now and was approached by the school board about the open coaching position at the high school." She paused, "He went back to Anderson County long enough to resign and pack up his things."

"He's been back for a few years now," Brooke pushed at Avery's arm. "If you came home more often than every five years, you'd know this already."

"It's of no consequence to me," Avery pushed the cup against her mouth, hoping her explanation sounded plausible.

"You went to senior prom with him," Paige said, as if Avery needed reminding. "I know you liked him. Never did say why you quit seeing him?"

"We were young," Avery blurted out before Paige could finish, hoping her excuse sounded plausible. "We just weren't compatible." Truth was, she did not know why they had never gone on a second date. And too much time had passed to ponder on it for any great amount of time. It simply was what it was, and it was in the past.

"Your cousin just came in, have you seen her yet?" Brooke asked, waving as a short, athletic woman in her mid-to-late thirties, made a beeline for their table.

"I left her a message that I was meeting you here at the bakery this morning," Avery answered before pushing to her feet to embrace the newcomer.

There were definite similarities between Avery and her cousin, but Avery was slightly taller and thinner, her body void of the musculature that came from farm life. In addition to running her household, Gaylin worked part time at Annetta's, the town's only florist. The years of packing and moving boxes from storage to the showroom, as well as delivering the arrangements, had left Gaylin bulkier and in better shape than Avery. Although, slightly older, Gaylin's beautiful graying hair was more indicative of Avery's paternal family tree, and she had eyes fashioned from pure crystals.

"Cousin!" Gaylin said once she was close enough to the table for her words to be heard. "Meant to come by Uncle Ward's last night but got caught up with some last-minute deliveries."

"Just as well," Avery slid into the booth as close against the wall as she could to accommodate Gaylin. "I fell asleep anyway, didn't even make it to dinner with my folks."

"City life has made you weak," Gaylin teased, turning the arrangement on the table towards her so she could get a better look.

"That's the truth," Avery agreed and indicated to the floral arrangement Gaylin was fiddling with, "one of yours?"

"I don't make them," Gaylin pushed it back to the center, "just deliver them." She stole a sip of water from one of the glasses on the table. "Aunt Patricia said you're home till after Christmas?"

"Yes, I'll hang around until we're sure the acquisition is finalized and head home after the New Year."

"Since Sami is attending UK, you could just stay?" Gaylin suggested, looking to Brooke and Paige for support. "Try your hand at writing again or whatnot?"

"I'm afraid that ship has left the port," Avery motioned to the server that she was ready for the check. "I've got some calls to make, I'll be at the café around one if anyone's available for lunch?"

"I've got meetings till 3," Brooke stood up and collected her purse. "Might be able to make dinner?"

"I've got a full schedule today," Paige explained. "It's good this place can run itself. I've been so busy with the Board; it's a busy time to be the mayor, especially with the Cove being sold and the renovations to the old footbridge."

"I heard the excavation was stopped," Gaylin stole another drink of water from the glass. "Something about Indian artifacts?"

"Yes," Brooke answered, "we're waiting for Brendan to finish his evaluation of what was dug up."

"How is Mr. Hall?" Avery asked, gathering her satchel on her shoulder and preparing to vacate the booth. "He must be like a hundred years old?" she joked, remembering her History teacher from high school, fondly.

"He's not that old," Paige joked. "And he was instrumental last year when they broke ground for the new elementary school. Was able to determine the old graves weren't Indian burial grounds and the project continued."

"That's good," Avery motioned to the others that she wanted out of the booth. "Hopefully, I'll run into him while I'm home."

"He's at the Blue House every Tuesday and Thursday when Griffin's band plays a few sets. He's a big fan of bluegrass music and seldom misses a performance." Paige moved closer to them before pausing and waiting for Brooke to join her.

"The Fall festival was amazing, Paige," Brooke added, making her way alongside her friend. "You and the volunteers did a fabulous job. I can't wait to see what you have planned for the Silent Night Celebration on Christmas Eve." She turned to Avery and pulled her into an embrace. "I'm so happy you're home to celebrate the holidays with us. It's been way too long."

"It has," Avery pulled away. "And I'm looking forward to it as well." She watched as her friends vacated the café. It was like being back in school and watching them as they walked down the hallway, arm to arm, heads close together in quiet conversation. "Going to stop by the bookstore and see if I can find a place to work till after lunch. There's too much commotion at Mom and Dad's with all that work going on."

"Going to be real nice when it's finished," Gaylin commented, pulling herself from the booth and collecting her keys. "I've got some deliveries to make. Not sure if I can meet for lunch but if any orders bring me back this way, I'll pop in."

"Sounds like a plan," Avery pulled her into an embrace and held on for what seemed like forever. "I have missed you, Cousin."

"And I missed you. If I'd have known all it would take to bring you home was to sell something, I'd asked Ms. Lorene to sell off one of those old buildings she used to store the floral supplies." Gaylin laughed, "how many cases of green Styrofoam does one actually need, anyway?"

"See you soon," Avery headed for the door, looking behind her once she was away from the café and into the street to determine if Gaylin had yet to exit. No doubt, by now she had struck up a conversation with one of the servers. It could be as long as an hour before the flowers were delivered to their rightful owners. There were no strangers in her cousin's world. She knew everyone in and about Green River Cove, where they lived and where they worked. Gaylin would say it was a side effect of her job, how her knowledge stemmed from the years of being the only delivery driver for Ms. Lorene's flower shop. But the truth was, she was a people person and had been since she was very young. Gaylin had always been able to strike up a conversation without any fanfare or invitation. It was just who she was. It was one of the things Avery loved most about her cousin and missed the many years of being so far away.

Chapter 3

It was in the air, and it was not the cool, crisp breeze clinging to the cusp of the Fall like a bell announcing dinner. It was different, as if the changes in store for Green River Cove had leaped over its fence and saturated her mind. She had only been in town overnight. Yet, it felt as if she had never left as if she had always been right there. It felt like home again and the thought was both comforting and worrisome, simultaneously.

Her home was in North Carolina, in a big, expensive house with more rooms than she needed. She would return to her corner office at Leopold Media where her life would once again settle into dinner with friends and book club once a month. She had not dated much at all since her divorce. Honestly, she had no desire to ride that bike again.

Her life was simple and as complete as she wanted it to be as she knocked upon the door of forty. Soon, her daughter would finish college and venture out into the world on her own. There would be another empty room in her big house. Perhaps, she should consider getting a dog?

For a split second, she considered perhaps the timing was right to explore writing again. But she slapped the thought away as quickly as it entered her mind. There was no need to go there. That chapter in her life was closed. Ironic, how if her life were to be a book, there would only be a few open chapters. Most of the others were closed tight as if the pages had been sealed with glue.

Matthew Leopold had been right when he suggested she close the bottling company deal from Green River Cove. It was a way, he had said, to ensure all the terms of the agreement were clear and concise. He did not want any hiccups with the acquisition. Avery knew the town and its people—who better to engage with them than one of their own?

When he had first used the analogy, her first thought was to question if his assessment was accurate. It had been many years since she thought of Green River Cove as home and even longer since she felt as if she belonged there. Even as a teenager, she had known she would leave the small town as soon as she could. The world outside of Green River Cove was big and she wanted an opportunity to see as much of it as possible. She could not wait to get out and she had, mere minutes after graduation.

In all the years, even after her writing career and marriage failed, there was never a time she considered returning to Kentucky. Yet, the notion danced upon her mind, yesterday during the drive and again this morning when she met her friends for breakfast. Laying roots in Green River Cove had been a rewarding and fulfilling experience for many people who were important in her life. Maybe if she had stayed, she would be as happy and content as those who did build their lives here? These were questions she would never have the answers for and no doubt, once she returned to North Carolina and fell into her old routines and patterns, the thought would disappear just as quickly. Once the sale of Cove Bottling was complete, there would be no reason to remain in Green River Cove, would there?

****

Trying to work at the bookstore had seemed like a good idea at the time but after nearly two hours and very little to show for it, she realized, working from the house may have been a better plan. The morning started out to be a productive one with only a few customers entering the store. Quickly, she became acclimated to the agitation of the bell over the doorway to announce entry and found that she hardly noticed it at all.

But once it was public knowledge that she was home, members of the community began to make appearances at the store to either purchase a copy of her book and have it signed or bring their copy and have it signed. Either way, she was inundated with visitors and conversation, many with people she had not interacted with in many years. Regardless of how little work she had completed, she was humbled at their interest in a book written so long ago.

By lunchtime, the bookstore had grown quieter, with most patrons opting to wander towards the bakery or café for a quick bite. Anxiously, she checked her watch; there would be no time for meeting anyone at the café today. She grabbed her phone and texted her friends and cousin how her morning had gotten away from her and was forgoing lunch today and hoping for an opportunity soon to get together.

She had no more than put her phone away when the buzz of a saw broke the stillness of the now quiet bookstore with such force it rattled the shelves of the conjoining wall. The hotel, she thought, someone had mentioned the old hotel had changed ownership and Rhem was now hoping to return it to its grandeur of the past. No doubt, he was the cause of the noise next door — or at the least, someone who worked with him? Perhaps, the ruckus was only temporary, and the construction might move to a calmer, quieter task, like painting?

In any event, she flipped the radio on, hoping music might drown out the annoying sounds coming from next door. All she could do was endure it; she could not leave the store. Her parents had taken the rare opportunity of enjoying lunch together for a change. Best she could hope for is that the annoyance was temporary or that her parents might return sooner instead of later.

After nearly an hour, without any hope of a silent reprieve, she celebrated in knowing her parents would be back from lunch soon and she could return to the house, maybe the barn would be a better choice? She closed her laptop, opting to catch up on emails once she returned to her parents' home. There was no point of trying to work, it sounded as if the workers next door were building an ark in what no doubt had been the main lobby. And there was just an inkling of curiosity beginning to grow, to see the inside of the old hotel and to see him.

How had all the years changed him? He was tall, a basketball player for the varsity team, with dark curly hair and a goofy, shy smile that was usually the first thing people noticed about him. What pattern of life had time placed upon him? Did she really want to know or simply remember him as he was and let him recall the younger, more vibrant version of herself?

Before she could contemplate it a minute longer, the door to the bookstore swung open, rocking the bell above the door with such force it sounded more like a fire alarm had been activated. And by looking at the surprised expression on his face, the alert might be an indication that one or both of them might need assistance soon.

It took a minute for him to realize she was minding the store and the only person he could address. There was no hope of finding cover behind one of the bookcases and letting one or both of her parents assist him. He was exposed, out in the open with nowhere to run.

"Hi," she saw his lips moving but was not close enough to hear his voice. It was not until he moved closer that she could make out his words over the pounding of her heart. "I heard you were home but didn't expect—"

"My parents went out to grab a bite to eat," she blurted as if her attendance in the store needed more justification. Her body was tense, like a trapped animal searching for an escape, and looking across the empty space between them, he was not fairing much better.

The years had been kind to him with a thick full head of hair cropped close against his head in direct contradiction to the long curly locks that once framed his face. And she could not be sure but there was just as much pepper as salt, giving him an air of distinction as if he would be most at home behind a podium in an auditorium full of college students. He was wearing faded jeans dusted with whatever medium he was working on in the hotel next door and the tips of his worn work boots were covered as well. What she could see of his shirt under the denim jacket was green, a nice compliment to his dark eyes which seem to beckon to her from across the room.

"I wanted to apologize for the noise," he finally said, taking a few steps further into the store before letting the door snap closed behind him. "Should be done with the lobby by the end of the week and can move deeper into the building. Won't be as audible over here." He paused and smiled. "You look just the same as when we were in school."

"Please," she blushed and pushed an errant strand of hair from her eyes. "I look my age and then some depending on what's going on with my daughter."

"Ms. Patricia talks about your daughter often," he smiled and closed the distance between them so that she could smell the fragrance of his cologne. It was thick and musky, and smelled expensive — unlike the brands he had worn in high school. A gift, she wondered, perhaps it was from someone special in his life, someone who enjoyed red wine and pasta over candlelight.

"She's a proud grandma, alright," Avery stepped away, hoping he couldn't read her thoughts and know what she had been pondering. "Your family alright?" It wasn't that she did not care to hear the status of his immediate family, but it was the only thing she could think to ask, the only thought she could hear over the pounding of her heart. It was as if it were going to burst from her chest.

"Lost my mom a few years ago but everyone else is doing well." His eyes were teary. "It's always hard, but especially this time of the year."

"I'm sorry for your loss," she moved closer and squeezed his hand, wishing she had remembered he had lost his mom. Paige had mentioned it over breakfast. "Your mother was always so nice to everyone, and she was your biggest fan, you know?"

"She was," he smiled, "I could always hear her cheering louder than everyone else in the crowd." He chuckled, "And remember that time the referee ejected her for heckling him?"

"Semi-finals in Jefferson County?" Avery laughed. "Yes, I thought he was going to have to toss all of us out of the gymnasium when he called that foul on you."

There was an awkward silence as their laughter faded, he moved uncomfortably from foot to foot before breaking the silence. "I should go, let you get back to work?"

"I wasn't doing much just waiting on my parents to return," her smile was warm and genuine. "It was really good seeing you again."

"Probably run into one another again while you're here?" he turned for the door.

"No doubt," should she add how she would pray for such an encounter?

He stopped at the door and turned back to her. "It's good to have you home. And if you want a tour of the hotel, just peck on the wall and I'll walk over."

"I might just do that," she promised, watching as he pulled open the door and stepped across the threshold.

"I hope you do," the door snapped closed behind him as she tried to discretely watch as he passed in front of the store window and disappeared from her view.

Well, she thought, that went better than she had imagined. Every time she played their encounter in her head, there had been remorse and resentment. Her imaginary self was angry and made no assumptions about what had or had not happened. His pretend self had begged for her forgiveness and pleaded for a second chance to be an important person in her life. To which she had simply dismissed his request and walked away, leaving him broken and ashamed on the pretend street.

She smiled, grateful for the outcome of the actual encounter. He seemed genuinely pleased to see her again. Green River Cove was a small town, and she knew if she just paced herself, their paths were sure to cross again. It was simply a matter of time.

****

And time was on her side when just a few days later, while waiting at the café for Brooke to bring the final draft of the acquisition papers, she was surprised to find him sliding into the empty chair across the table from her.

Before she could inquire, he informed her how he had just come from Brooke's office and how she was running a few minutes late. Mostly because she had been instrumental in having the hotel declared a historic landmark. In addition to protecting it from any future demolition, the declaration afforded him access to a minimal monetary state grant. It wasn't much, he assured her as he waved to the server and pointed to Avery's coffee cup as a signal that he, too, would like a cup, but on a high school coach's salary, every little bit helped.

Over the next ten minutes, he explained to her how happy he had been with the coaching proposal from the local high school that was presented to him. And how much he missed living in Green River Cove. There was little chance he would ever consider leaving again.

He waited for the server to refill Avery's cup and set a new cup on the table in front of him before continuing on. His ex-wife, he explained, was an amazing person and although he was grateful for knowing her, he had known long before it ended that they weren't compatible as a couple. They had always been better as friends.

Was that how he had felt about her when they were dating? Had he known the night of their prom as they danced across the gymnasium floor meticulously decorated to look like the deck of a massive ship, that they would not make it together as a couple? Was that why he had dropped her like a hot potato before the week's end?

"Thanks, Rhem," Brooke came to an abrupt stop at his side, dropping her satchel in the empty space on the table between them. She turned quickly to Avery, "Sorry, the call with Leopold ran longer than I thought it would." She watched as Rhem bid his farewell and took his exit, promising to provide Avery with a quick tour of the hotel whenever she was ready to see it.

"Why are meetings still going on? Isn't signing the document simply an exercise?" Avery asked, her frustration evident by way she sat in the chair and folded her arms over her chest.

"The document is partially executed," Brooke explained. "Patterson signed earlier this morning; I've sent the documents overnight to North Carolina for Matthew Leopold's signature. Should be back in a few days and we can start the ownership transfer process."

"What did they want to discuss today?"

Brooke flipped through several pages of a small notebook, reading her notes. "They had questions about the existing agreement with the vendor Cove purchases glass bottles from, the graphic artist who does the illustrations, and the costs associated with cleaning and reusing the bottles."

"That's it?"

"Other random things associated with the care and maintenance of the building, the resources currently employed to manage the factory, and things like that."

"All these things were discussed at the discovery meeting. You were there," Avery's brows arched as they emphasized her confusion.

"I know," Brooke dropped several cubes of sugar into her coffee. "I think they are just crossing all their

T's." She pushed the cup to her lips and blew across the top. "So, what were you and Rhem talking about?"

"Just making conversation," Avery took a big gulp and waited for the barrage of questions she knew would be forthcoming. She was mildly surprised when none were forthcoming. "Since it will be a few days before the fully executed document is back to us, I thought I'd make myself useful and help Paige with some of Silent Night Celebration tasks."

"That sounds like a wonderful idea, and I know she can use the help." Brooke's expression grew sad, her eyes tearing up at the thought of whatever was on her mind. "Will be a real hard one for us this year with Patrick being deployed and all. Will be the first year I haven't had both my boys home for Christmas."

"I can only imagine," Avery reached across the table and took her hand. "If there's anything I can do, let me know?"

"Is Samantha spending Christmas with you or your ex?" Brooke asked, her words filled with empathy.

"Me," Avery smiled, seeing her child in her mind's eye. "And I'm looking forward to spending it here with her in Green River Cove."

"You and Rhem seem to be picking up where you left off after graduation." Brooke dropped the net. Although the girls had known each other most of their adolescent life, they knew very little of one another as adults, especially now when the images looking back from the mirror each morning showed signs of middle aging. Why Avery and Rhem quit seeing one another was still a mystery to Brooke too.

"He's being polite and welcoming," Avery offered, pulling the folder from Brooke's hand and flipping anxiously through the pages. "You sure there's nothing in here I need to be concerned about?"

"Not that I'm aware of," Brooke advised. "Milby wants to sell, and Leopold wants to buy. Very straightforward." She indicated towards the folder. "And the sale is broken into two parcels like you asked. Although, I don't understand why Leopold wants the land behind the bottling company too. It's his money."

"If the National campaign is as successful as I've projected, we will need a larger dock and more trucks. And I'm expecting some expansion to be required of the warehouse itself, at some time in the future." Avery leaned back in her chair, pleased to be a part of breathing new life into the old bottling plant. Rush was more than just a soda to the community—it was important in ways other than financial. It had been a prominent place in the town's history, and it felt good to know she had played a part of ensuring it remained a piece of its future. "Mrs. Sandige would have been pleased to know that small strip of land she hoped to pass down to her son would play such a vital role in Green River Cove."

"She would have," Brooke laughed. "And it's a fine way to honor his memory as well as his service to the country." There was a pause as both women paid their respects to a man they never met, although, knew intimately through the stories told by his aged mother many times over the years.

Brooke snatched the folder back from Avery. "Stop changing the subject. What has Rhem said? Anything about why he broke it off so abruptly?"

"We have steered clear of any discussion around prom, dating, or dancing," Avery dropped a handful of bills on the center of the table. "Probably for the best, was a long time ago."

"Don't give me that," Brooke stood and gathered her things. "I know you; how many times has it crossed your mind since you returned home?"

"Once or twice," Avery followed her to the door, hoping Brooke would not see through the lie. "But I don't think it matters so much anymore. We've both moved on and are in different phases of life. I think we can both settle on just being friends."

"That's too bad. I thought, maybe, after he returned home and your divorce was final—"

"Don't be ridiculous, we live four hundred miles away from one another. Not to mention we haven't spoken in nearly twenty years."

"That's just geography," Brooke smiled, holding the door open and motioning for Avery to exit first. "The rest is simply chemistry."

Chapter 4

The weather outside was cooler, and along the ground thick piles of damp leaves pocked the pathway leaving a design that resembled a checkerboard, of sorts. Although, the sun was partially visible as it dodged in and out of the thick, milky clouds, it was by far the cloudiest day of the season, one that signaled a change was coming. It was the first day that felt like Fall.

The various vehicles, cars as well as work trucks, parked irregularly in the dirt lot near the recreation center as well as the front door propped open were sure indicators that something was going on inside. It was filled, wall to wall, with volunteers of varying ages, each bursting with excitement at the task that lie ahead of them. Paige had seen to it that the groups of teenagers, adults, and skilled workers were distributed evenly among the many stations in preparation for the Silent Night Celebration. It was less than three weeks away; there was much to be done.

Christmas in Green River Cove

Behind the recreation center, Griffin's crew of construction workers moved quickly, nailing and bolting large sections of lumber marked from previous years together. Many vending stands would be required for the evening and as each year past, it seemed as if the number he and his team put together continued to grow.

Inside, representatives of the various churches gathered around their stations, assembling centerpieces and garden-like arches alive with the yellow, brown, red, and orange colors of Fall. Not far away, large blocks of white Styrofoam were being fashioned into various sizes of snowmen while a select few danced in and around the snow people dressing them in fashionable gender appropriate winter clothes.

All the way to the back, taking up nearly the entire back quarter of the center, were dozens of bins and boxes, tops ajar with strands of green garland hanging over the sides like ropes. There were ornaments of every color, big and smaller, solid and glittering like the sun, piled as high as the bins would allow. Nearby, high school students gathered around several tables, wrapping boxes of every size and shape with Christmas paper of all colors. Back near the front door, several tables were pushed together to accommodate a large schematic of what would be the Silent Night Celebration. At the front of the tables, Paige stood, hands on her hips assessing the progress as if she were the Captain and the recreation center, her ship.

"Are you sure you're at the right spot?" Avery asked, smiling as Rhem peeled his coat off and made his way to where she sat pushing artificial flowers into table-size wicker cornucopias. "You never struck me as the artistic type." She pointed over her shoulder with her thumb. "The construction teams are out back."

"Haha," he moved to the same side of the table as she was. "What can I do that I won't mess up?"

"The construction team is—" her words were flat, but it was obvious by her body language, she was pleased that they were working together. Although, there was little probability that it had happened by chance. It had the fragrance of Paige written all over it. And she could tell by his expression, Rhem knew it as well.

She handed him a pair of wire cutters and one of the plastic fall floral bunches stacked in the table's center. "Cut these into individual strands and leave the stalk as long as you can. I'll cut off what I don't need."

He nodded and set his attention to the task as she had described to him. She did not realize he had separated all of the bushes into single stems and stacked them by like across the table in front of her until he clapped his hands together and asked for the next task. And she gave him many over the next hour and a half. By the end of the afternoon, they had completed all of their station tasks and moved to assist an older couple at another table assembling artificial mini Christmas trees.

Christmas in Green River Cove

By the end of the evening, she found herself walking with him to end of the street to enjoy a quick dinner before heading back to her parents' house. She was not sure why she had accepted his offer, her lips had already formed a response of refusal, when her head nodded an acceptance as if it had a will of its own. There was no point in starting something, she wasn't even sure what to call it, with him. Her time in Green River Cove would be coming to an end soon. And she was not a fan of long-distance relationships. Besides, they had had their chance at being a couple. That ship had sailed and sunk. It was laying on the bottom of an ocean somewhere, probably not too far from where the Titanic had gone down.

Still, there was something comforting about his smile, the way his dark eyes lit up when he leaned in closer to better hear what she had to say, and the way his hand touched the small of her back every time he led her through an open door. It brought back the memories of summer picnics at the lake with friends and Fall hayrides that signaled the beginning of the new school year.

Her last year of high school had been something akin to a fairytale with Rhem as her Prince Charming and his Grandpa's old seventy-seven Chevy as their chariot. And although, much had changed in the many years since she had left Green River Cove, other things had not. There was no denying her feelings. Rhem was her first love, and there was no need to deny that she still had feelings for him.

****

The walk to the café took only a minute or two. Yet, with the silence between as they neared an outside table with a quaint checkered tablecloth draped across it and a thick, heavy vase of Fall flowers, the distance seemed greater. She felt the fatigue as if she had just finished a marathon.

"You want coffee or wine?" he asked, waiting beside the chair across the table with his hand resting on the chair back.

"How about some warm cider, instead?" She pointed to the placard on one of the adjoining tables and slid into the empty chair across from where he stood. This was not a date, her mind screamed. There was no need to pretend it was anything other than two old friends catching up. He had made that decision for them both, years earlier. And there was no time machine to go back and right the wrong. Besides, her heart echoed back, she had not thought about high school prom or Rhem in many years. She had met a good man who gave her an amazing daughter. Maybe things had worked out the way fate intended. Seeing him again was just as it seemed, a reunion of old friends.

If he was disappointed she had not taken the seat he intended, he gave no indication. Instead, he slid into the chair and dropped his hands atop the table as if he was readying his end of the table for finger football and it was her turn. "Good idea, I haven't had a chance to stop by yet, been so busy with the hotel."

"What made you want to renovate it?" she laughed, peeling her coat off and draping it across the back of her chair. "You're a basketball coach."

"I know my way around a hammer and saw," he smiled, the light in his eyes dancing off the streetlamps as if they were on fire. "I was in charge of the Junior float committee for homecoming."

"I see." There was a pause as they waited for the server to deliver two steaming cups of cider to the table. The aroma assaulted her senses before her lips made contact with the cup, igniting a recollection of memories of pep rallies where the fire burned so high into the heavens, the stench of ash scattered for miles and lasted for many days. "And then you went away to college and haven't picked up a hammer since?"

"I like physical work; it breaks the mental stresses of coaching." He took a long sip from the cup and sat it down gently on the table. "I built a deck and gazebo at my place in Anderson County." He wrung his hands back and forth against the table, a gesture she recalled from his day of playing basketball. It had been part of his process to calm himself down before and during a game.

"Kelly, my ex-wife, always had a honey-do list." He pulled his hands apart and dropped them against his lap. "And I enjoyed the work, so we had a nice-looking place, inside and outside."

"I'll have to take you up on that offer to tour the hotel and judge your work for myself," changing the subject seemed to be a necessity. No doubt, the next series of discussion would be for her to ask about his failed marriage or him to inquire of hers. She wasn't ready to share those details, yet, with anyone. And by the look on his ashen face, he was regretting mentioning his ex-wife or the house that was part of the life they had once shared.

It was as if their table was encapsulated within a time capsule, as if they were back at Green River High School and had never left town. It was something she had taken for granted, the peacefulness and contentedness that had been a part of the life they had once known. She liked that in Green River Cove she could simply be Avery, a want to be writer. And he was Rhem, a boy who dreamed of playing in the NBA. In this space and time, there were no failed relationships, equitable distribution of common property, or custody agreements. It was him and her and she felt young again.

****

The hour was late by the time the plates were cleared away from the table. Yet, it felt as if she had just sat down at the table and ordered the apple cider. The café, too, had gotten busier, as several folks loitered nearby waiting for a table to open up inside. Twice, she looked around, thinking maybe they should pay the bill and offer the table to someone waiting, but each time, the longing look in his eyes prompted her to pretend she had not noticed those waiting for a table outside under the stars.

Rhem motioned for the server to refill their empty cider cups and waved off the server's offer of dessert. Once the cups were filled and the steam lifted like fog from the space between them, it was hard not to notice the change in his temperament, how anxious he had become. He swallowed, waiting as the saliva crawled down his throat and the breath he was holding was expelled.

"I've been hoping we could talk," the words came out so quickly it was obvious he was having second thoughts once the statement was out in the open.

"We've talking for the last two hours," Avery hoped he would take the hint and retreat the conversation back to a safe topic like the acquisition or his renovation of the hotel.

"I mean about prom," his words were nearly a whisper.

"Rhem," she dropped the cloth napkin atop the table and motioned to the server she wanted the check. "I'd hoped we could focus on life in the present and not harp on the past?"

"Avery," he pulled her hand into his. "Seeing you again has meant so much to me. I'd forgotten so much about that year."

"Let it go," she pulled her hand from his. "It was a long time ago and to be honest I've not thought about it in many years."

"That's unfortunate," his body language was rigid, as if his torso was made of stone. "Because I thought about you a lot, right up until I met Kelly."

"I'm happy you found someone, 'cause I did too and I have an amazing daughter—"

"Your daughter is away at college. And Craig nor Kelly is in our lives anymore. We've been given a second chance." The legs of the chair scraped against the concrete of the outside patio as he pushed himself away from the table. "I've forgiven you for—"

"You've forgiven me?" she jumped to her feet. "You forgave me?" she repeated again to ensure she had heard him correctly. "For what, going to senior prom with you and then getting dumped?"

"Dumped?" he looked around to where several onlookers were paying close attention to their conversation. "I didn't dump you," he moved closer, no doubt hoping he could guide her into a more private area.

"Obviously, this was a mistake," she waved her hands between them across the table as if to emphasize she meant him and her as a couple, enjoying dinner. "We are arguing over something that happened twenty years ago." She tossed a handful of bills onto the middle of the table, more than enough to cover the tab. "I have an early day tomorrow. Thank you for the invitation."

"Wait," he stepped into her path, effectively impeding her exit. "Please don't leave. I don't believe in coincidences. Fate is giving us a second chance to get it right this time."

"I have to go," she stepped past him, hoping she could get out of the restaurant and away from prying eyes. She could feel the tears building behind her eyes and feel the tremble as her lips began to quiver. Avery did not want to break down in public but would have no problem crying into the pillow once she made the trip to her parents' home. "Drive safely."

"Avery?" he pleaded again, following her only as far as the wrought iron of the patio's gate.

But she was gone, disappearing into the night, like an apparition on a dark and stormy night. And there was little left for him to say.

****

"Did he say exactly what he was forgiving you for?" Paige asked, sliding cozily into the booth next to Avery and pushing a full cup of coffee into Brooke's hands. "I mean, didn't he dump you?"

Avery nodded, eyeing the last powdered sugar covered chocolate croissant on the ceramic platter in the center of the table. It had taken hours for her to fall asleep after retiring upstairs to her bedroom. There had been little opportunity for small talk as her father had gone to bed hours earlier and her mother was following suit when Avery's key in the door had caused her to pause and offer a greeting before following joining Ward in calling it a night.

As a result, the ticking of the old clock on her bedroom wall was the only engagement Avery had enjoyed since leaving Rhem at the restaurant. She pondered his accusation over and over until her head was little more than a throbbing and painful mass of neurons and transmitters. And the ache extended all the way down her neck and shoulders before it pummeled the channels of her heart.

The many years of not knowing why he had dumped her had been bad enough, but to hear him, in his own words, say he forgave her was just too much. And what had there been to forgive her for? She had spent her final Summer at home, alone in her room, reliving prom night in an attempt to determine what she had done wrong. What had happened that caused him to push her away without as much as even a goodbye, good luck, or see you later?

"He did do the dumping," Brooke answered before Avery could. "I mean he didn't call or anything. Weren't you supposed to go out again the next weekend?"

"Yes, we were," Avery wrapped her fingers around the sugary pastry and pulled it onto her plate. She was a stress eater; always had been, everyone close to her knew that.

"And he just fell off the face of the Earth?" Paige was outraged, reliving the humiliation over again like the good friend she was. "Why would he blame you?"

"Obviously, there's been some kind of miscommunication," Brooke's words were calming, like one of those tapes that might play in a therapist's office. "Did you think that maybe he might have explained what he meant if you'd given him the opportunity to?" She swallowed a couple of sips of coffee before adding, "I mean don't you want to know what he's talking about it?"

"No," Avery pushed the saucer with the pastry remnants away, letting it scrape against the wooden table loudly. "I don't. I haven't thought about him or that dance in a very long time." She pushed herself from the booth as if the cushions were on fire. "I can't get distracted by all this. I've got a few more weeks here in Green River Cove and then I'm back to North Carolina. The chances of seeing Rhem after that are slim to none." She pulled her satchel over her shoulder as if preparing for war. "I just need to keep my distance until this deal is done and then everything goes back the way it was."

"And that's a good thing?" Brooke asked, exchanging glances with Paige.

"Yes," Avery fought back the tears. "It is. We had our chance, and we blew it. One or both of us, it really doesn't matter at this point." She forced a smile and wiped anxiously at the tears clinging to the ledge of her eyelids. "I'll catch up with you guys for an early dinner later, if I can."

"Are you working from the bookstore again?" Paige asked, gathering the cups and saucer into her arms.

"As long as it doesn't get complicated." Avery made her way to the door. "I don't think he'll walk over again after last night."

"You can always use the empty office next to mine," Brooke offered, dropping a handful of bills on the table. "Let me know so I can let my assistant know you're coming."

"Of course, thanks," Avery disappeared through the door casting a final apologetic glance towards Paige and Brooke before the door snapped closed behind her. She only had a few documents to review, and she could return home to her parents' place. Even with all the construction, it was a better option than running into Rhem again.

Chapter 5

W orking from her parents' house had not panned out exactly as she had planned. Although, the general contractor's vehicle in the driveway was an immediate lift to her spirit, she could not help but wonder where the other workers were. From the stack of pressure treated lumber stacked in the side yard to the scaffolding locked into place upon the front porch, it was obvious the renovations were ongoing. No doubt, her parents were taking the revisions seriously. Avery could not recall a time in the house's history where such extensive cosmetic surgery was ongoing.

She nearly collided with Griffin, Paige's husband and general contractor for the project, at the front door as she was entering upon his exit. With his attention focused on the folded set of blueprints under his nose, he did not realize he had company until they were face to face.

"Sorry," she stepped to the side to allow him his exit. "You working solo, today?"

His smile was wide as he pushed his glasses higher atop the bridge of his nose and paused just outside the front door that led to the porch. "We're way ahead of schedule, gave the guys the afternoon off." He smacked the blueprint with his calloused hand. "We'll be done in plenty of time for—" He paused, his eyes wide, almost frantic as if he had forgotten what they were talking about.

"In time for what?" she asked, moving closer to him. Maybe Griffin should have taken the afternoon off as well, he sure did seem out of sorts.

"Christmas," he smiled, moving towards the steps. "I promised Patricia we'd have the place in order long before she needed to pull out the Christmas decorations." It was no secret that her Mom loved decorating for the holidays, all the holidays, but especially Christmas. Growing up, her parents' home had been "that" house with lights adorning every window and awning. Garland and bells embellished every hedge and ornamental bush. Even the trees were ornamented as high within its branches as Ward could manage.

"You don't want to mess with Christmas, Griffin." Avery slid past him into the house. "And your crew is doing a wonderful job. I can't believe how great this old place is looking." She slid out of her jacket and draped it over the coat rack. "Will look like a completely new place when you're done."

"That's the plan," he joked, pushing the blueprints up under his arm. "Enjoy the peace and quiet this afternoon. My crew will be back bright and early tomorrow morning."

"I will," she waved him off, letting the screen door close but leaving the outside door open to the Fall elements. Although, it was a little on the cool side, its breeze would be refreshing as she studied the papers Leopold Media had sent over to Brooke's firm.

The sound of Griffin's truck as it pulled away was comforting. It had been many years since she had the place all to herself. It was like having coffee with an old friend.

****

Accidental, she would tell herself later on, when it was all said and done. That was how she would remember the moment. Innocent was the other word that came to mind. There were three expensive pens in her satchel and none of them seemed to be working. She had not intended to snoop through the drawers in the kitchen, it had just kind of happened. And once the genie was out of the bottle, there was no pushing her back inside.

Her parents were planning to sell the house. The objective evidence was there in her hand, a preliminary contract with a local realtor effective the week after the new year. And if that was not enough of a shock, they were selling the bookstore too.

****

The burden of having the information was weighing heavy upon her heart. And being alone in the house was making it worse. She needed to talk to someone who could help her understand why, after all these years, her parents would want to abandon their home to strangers.

Travel, the rational, less emotional portion of her brain proposed. They had always dreamed of traveling to faraway, exotic places. Yet, other than an intermittent trip to Louisville during the Christmas season and upon the resumption of school, Avery could not recall them venturing far outside of Green River Cove. Still, the proof was in her hand, a seven-page executed agreement to put both the house and bookstore in the hands of strangers after the holidays.

Christmas, she fought back the tears. This would be their last Christmas Eve in the house she had grown up in. It would be the final morning of awaking on Christmas day to the hearty, greasy, aroma of turkey roasting in the oven. Her mother preferred to cook the turkey overnight, after everyone had gone to bed on Christmas Eve. This allowed her the opportunity to focus on the side dishes and desserts, ensuring every dish made it to the table at the precise temperature. Hot food hot, and cold food cold. It was her motto, her mission, one Avery had not yet mastered.

****

Her parents showed no surprise as the bell above the room shook as if angry while Avery marched across the threshold of the bookstore's entrance. Was there disappointment and confusion painted upon her face like a tattoo? She had never been very inept at hiding things from her mother. Somehow Patricia always knew when something was amiss. Still, neither she nor Ward broached the subject. If they were aware, they said nothing and gave no indication of the secret they had been harboring. And she was not going to give anything up either. They would tell her when they were ready.

She watched as they gathered up their belongings and handed her the keys, grateful that she had offered to close up the bookstore for them again. It had been many years since they had enjoyed so much time together as a couple, Avery knew they were grateful for the opportunity. Perhaps, if she or her siblings had made the offer more frequently over the years, they would not be looking to sell the family home and close that chapter of their life.

Although the time passed quickly, she could not wrap her thoughts around much else except the upcoming sale of the family home and business. Maybe she should have alerted them that she had inadvertently discovered the agreement with the relator? Perhaps, then she might have some of the answers she sought. Instead, she sat, chin propped up upon her hands as if she were back in History class in high school, listening to the teacher as she discussed the civil war but not actually hearing anything she had said. It sounded like the audio background during one of those old Peanuts cartoons when an adult spoke. Blah, Blah, Wa, Wa. There were words, sounds even — yet, none made any sense.

She could not be sure how many times her phone rang before she acknowledged the shrill scream it made as it echoed throughout the empty store — just that she answered it before the caller hung up. Sandra, her assistant's voice was clear and upbeat as usual, yet tinged with an anxiousness she tried hard to conceal. What could possibly be going on back at Leopold Media that could warrant the tension in Sandra's words as well as a trip back to North Carolina on the next available flight.

Avery checked her watched and nodded as if Sandra was in the store and could see Avery nodded in agreement. The next flight, she considered, hoping the meeting with Leopold and the board would not take very long. The Silent Night Festival was only a week away, she was excited to participate in the event, even without Rhem's accompaniment. It was as if Sandra had read her mind and knew the deliberation that was ongoing. Just for a quick meeting, she added, noting how Avery would fly in and out on the same day.

It was human nature to inquire if everything was alright and Sandra's response was predictable. She had no information other than Matthew and the board had called an emergency meeting as soon as Avery could get back to North Carolina. There was no choice but to wait and see. No doubt, it would be a long night.

Closing time came quickly despite Avery's anxiety around her trip back to North Carolina in the morning. On a positive note, her work-related dilemma provided a temporary reprieve from worrying over the upcoming sale of her parents' home. She had barely thought of it since Sandra's call and the thought left her with a deep boding sense of guilt. How quickly she had fallen back into a routine of prioritizing work above all else.

The residual aroma of pumpkin spice and cinnamon that hung in the air had been a welcomed change since returning home to Green River Cove. Coming home had been akin to never leaving, sort of. For the last week, she was simply Avery, a want-to-be writer who saw little of life beyond the small town she called home. Here, there were no budget meetings, market analysis, or requests for proposals—only the scent of fresh bread from the bakery and the sound of the dry leaves being crushed under her boots as they split into microscopic particles that would be swept away by the cool winds of Fall. It was both a blessing and a curse, living on the line between the two very different worlds and feeling as if she belonged in both and neither at the same time.

****

By the time six o'clock rolled around, the world on the other side of the store's glass window was dark, with only the light from the streetlamps to mark the route from one business to the next. Although, the refrigerator at her parents' house contained an appropriate array of foods appropriate for her dinner, she was not in the mood for leftovers or to eat alone. She checked her watch, noting there was more than enough time for a quick bite at the café before heading back to her parents' and preparing for her flight back to North Carolina. Morning would come soon enough, there was no point in worrying about what might have prompted her return and it would be evident soon enough.

The bookstore lock had always been tricky to secure. It was as if a certain skill was required to both hold the key at a specific angle with one hand and twist it in synchronized succession with the other. In any event, it was a skill she apparently did not possess one hundred percent of the time. Tonight was no exception. She had tried unsuccessfully, several times, to trip the lock and lock it into place. It was no use, the lock remained unsecured, and she had run out of options.

"Need a hand?" his words echoed across the walkway from where he stood near the closest lamppost. It was obvious, he had kept his distance as to not frighten her.

"I'm going to wait a second or two and take another stab at it." She exhaled, not bothering to turn around. Between finding out about her parents' house and being called back to North Carolina for an as of yet undisclosed reason, she had little time to invest in the dysfunctional lock.

"Here," he moved closer, pushing his lean body between the door and her body. "It's a temperamental lock. Your Dad's been aiming to replace it for months now but can't seem to remember to pick up a lock at the hardware store."

"Don't bother," her words were soft as was her response as she stepped away and allowed him better access to the door; seemed to be a contradiction. "I've been able to get it locked before." She breathed, "Guess, my fingers and my head aren't on the same page."

"No worries," he smiled as the lock snapped loudly into place and he dropped the key back into her hand. She knew by his body language, he was pacing himself, waiting for an opportunity to reopen the discussion about the dance and who was to blame for what.

But he did not. Instead, he retreated back towards the lamppost and leaned the full weight of his long body against it. "Are you heading home for the night?"

"I am," there was little need to augment her response. If she mentioned she was planning to have dinner before retreating to her parents', it might open the door for him to accompany her. She did not want to argue about it anymore. It was all she could do to manage the stress of her meeting tomorrow. Worrying about a heart that was broken twenty years ago seemed like a waste. Even after apologies were made and accepted, it would change nothing. His life was here and hers was not.

"Can I show you something?" He pushed himself away from the hard surface of the pole, his eyes reflecting off the light as if they were on fire. The years melted away like ice as she recollected his smile and how complete it had felt to dance in his arms. It took all of her reserve to drag herself back to the present time, a moment when the wall between them was tall and wide.

"Some other time?" she lied. She had no intention of engaging with him in any way, anytime soon.

"Will only take a minute," he pointed next door to the hotel. "I would really like for you to see it." He moved closer and pleaded, "Please?"

"Alright," she dropped the keys in her pocket. "But I've got an early flight out tomorrow —"

"You're leaving already?" His forward motion ceased, his face overflowing with disappointment. "I thought you'd be here through the New Year?"

"I am," she slid past him and stopped near the door, waiting as Rhem flipped the lock and pushed open the door of the hotel. "Just a quick trip there and back for a meeting."

The room illuminated in a soft, warm light just as the door behind them snapped closed, and Avery fought to catch her breath. The richness of the wood floors and the mahogany mantle that bordered the fireplace against the farthest wall was like looking into a portal to a time long since passed. There was a glass chandelier in the center of the room that reflected the light from an oversized wall mirror. And floral wallpaper with rows of tiny flowers so precise, it was as if the gap between the two had been designed specifically for it.

Rhem had a keen eye for recreating the time period and it was easy to imagine the room as it was during the hotel's heyday. She had to admit she was envious she would not be around to see the finished project. It would be like traveling back into time once the furniture and window treatments were placed.

"It's beautiful," she ran her hand along the surface of the counter at the check-in area. "You should be so proud." She spun around to enjoy another look at the expanse of the room. "It's going to be amazing when it's done." She pointed down the corridor, "What's down there?"

"The hallway leads to what will be the main event venue," he smiled. "We can host parties of up to about two hundred. And there will be a smaller one on the top floor that will hold about a hundred. There's a balcony on the backside that will be really nice when I'm done."

"What about the floors upstairs?" she wandered across the room where the lighting was not as good, and the room was cast in half shadows. "What's your plan there?"

"The floor plan right now for the second floor includes four one-room efficiencies." He waved towards the stairs. "The place will be much further along by the time you return, hopefully before next Christmas?"

"Four rooms, like hotel rooms?" Her words were softer as the distance between them grew until she stopped outside of a ridiculously small room just on the other side of the door.

"More like an apartment," he clarified. "Like one of those New York lofts where everything is right there in a single space with a bathroom." He followed behind her, stopping as close behind her as he dared.

"Have you ever been to New York?" she peered into the darkened room.

"Once for a tournament but all I could afford was a room at the Quality Inn. You?"

"Many times but mostly on the company and usually at the Marriott or the Hilton," she disappeared into the darkness of a tiny room, just off the main area. "What's the plan for this one?"

He stepped in behind her, balancing as if he were walking a tightwire. The room was barely large enough for a desk and a chair, maybe a small bookcase or two on the wall across from where the desk would be placed. It was without a window or wash area. It was, by all accounts, a glorified coat closet. "The realtor believes it was probably used by the telephone operator to connect calls coming into the hotel to a specific room." He flipped the light on and turned to face her. "It's not big enough for much else." His body fell against the wall, and he folded his arms against his chest. "What would you do with it?"

"I don't know," she smiled. "Not much you can do, it's so small."

"You must have some thoughts?"

"A writing room," she smiled, walking away and stopping at the wall deepest into the room. "I'd put a few bookcases over there, an antique desk here with an old wooden chair, and one of those old lamps with a pull string."

"A writing room?" he rubbed his chin. "You mean like a library?"

"No," she returned to the threshold of the room and turned back to look upon it, in its entirety. "A writing room where you'd sit and watch the people come and go and simply imagine where they came from or where they might be headed."

"Why'd you stop writing?" His words were tender, his eyes glazed as if he had been drinking.

"I was a one hit wonder," she looked away, wishing there was something else to focus on, somewhere else she could look. His proximity was making it hard for her to think, to focus on her words. And the room was suddenly warmer as if a fire had been lit in the fireplace, but the hearth was stone cold.

"I read it," he moved closer, "but that wasn't my favorite book. I liked the short stories much better. They were a better reflection of who you really are."

"Who I am?" she repeated, suddenly irritated with him. Who was he to presume to know her, really know her, especially after he had forfeited any right at having an actual relationship?

"Yes," he whispered.

"I don't want to argue with you, Rhem." Her words were flat, spirit deflated, and she was suddenly very tired. Perhaps, she would forego dinner and just go back to her parents'.

"Nor I you," he exhaled. "I know what you said to Katherine and Donna about prom night with me."

"What?" she really had no idea what he was talking about. Had he just mentioned two friends from high school with whom she had casual familiarity? They ran in different circles than she did but were friendly to one another. They had a single class, Literature, together.

"I heard you, a few days after prom when they asked you if you had a good time with me and if we were going out again." In a flash, his demeanor changed. He was a little boy again, one who was chosen last again at recess. His face was ashen, pale; his eyes were sad.

She had to think hard before an incident matching what he had described came to her mind. Truth was it was so insignificant at the time; she had given it very little thought. It was not that she was not friends with Katherine and Donna. She was, but not to the extent that she would be willing to share anything personal with either of them. Those types of discussions occurred with Brooke and Paige. Both Katherine and Donna had a tendency to gossip and exaggerate the details of any encounter to one that better suited whatever story they were sharing. There was no way she wanted either of them to know anything personal that may or may not have happened with Rhem during prom night.

"I don't know what you're talking about. I wouldn't have told either of them anything, good or bad, that may or may not have happened that night. It was none of their business." She paused, the fire in her gut burning her throat and straining her words. "It was no one's business but ours."

"I heard you," he reiterated. "I was on the other side of the room divider. I had Spanish, remember."

Room divider? She flipped through the memories like file folders in a metal cabinet. Yes, Literature, Spanish, Civics, and Algebra were conducted in one large room, segregated by dividers into four separate rooms, each under the direction and supervision of a designated educator. She and Rhem only had one class together, History, and it was towards the end of the school day.

The week of classes after prom were little more than an exercise in attendance for the Senior class, as most of the grades had to be finalized a few days before graduation. As a result, they wandered through the hallways, from one class to the other, doing little more than socializing and playing card games in the time normally allotted to a specific class.

Avery remembered bits and pieces of that last week of high school, the way one might recollect an old black and white film. And images of the conversation she'd had with Katherine and Donna were there on the edges of her memory, like a piece of paper whose edges had been burned away into irregular, jagged pieces of the whole. She remembered being asked if he had kissed her. And thinking to herself how there was no way she was telling either of them anything about her special night. It was hers and his, and she was not going to share.

"They asked you if you liked me and would go out with me again," he bit his lip. "And you blew it off like it was nothing." He looked away. "I couldn't wait to go out with you again and when I heard you talking with them. I realized you didn't feel the same way." He exhaled a long breath. "You should have just told me the truth."

"You don't understand," Avery walked towards the door. "That's not what happened, not at all. I had an amazing night and I thought it was the beginning of a wonderful journey with you." She stopped at the door. "I had no idea, our first real date, would also be our last."

"But I heard what you said—" he took her arm.

"I wasn't going to share how I really felt with them," she blurted out. "It was private between us. I said what I said to get them to move on to a juicier story and they did just that." She wiped at the tears that threatened to fall down her cheeks. "I'd forgotten you had class on the other side of the partition. Didn't even remember it till now." She fought back a laugh. "All this time, I thought you dumped me."

"And I thought you dumped me," he added, his eyes wide and disbelieving.

"I have to go," she reached for the door.

"Wait," he grabbed for her hand. "We have to talk, this changes everything."

"Not really," she kissed his cheek. "Was a long time ago, Rhem. Neither of us are those people anymore."

"We don't have to be those people, Avery," he swallowed. "We can be better versions of the people we were."

"I'm only here for another week or so and my life resumes in North Carolina." She waved behind her. "And you've built an amazing legacy here."

"And neither of those scenarios could hold a candle to the life we might have had together?"

"I'll see you when I get back," she opened the door, visibly shaking as the cold air rushed across the threshold. "Thank you for sharing this with me. I think it's good we both got some closure."

"Can we talk about this tomorrow, over dinner?" He followed behind her, pulling the door closed behind him.

"I don't think so," she bundled the coat as tightly around her body as she could. "But I'm sure we'll run into one another in town and there's the Silent Night Celebration."

"If that's what you want, sure," he did not try to hide his disappointment.

"It is," she forced a smile, taking large strides towards her car. Somewhere between leaving the bookstore and touring the hotel, she had lost her appetite. There was nothing she wanted more than to fall into a hot bath and then jump into bed. The flight to North Carolina would be a welcomed distraction. What he had told her had cut her to the core. All these years, he had nursed a broken heart as well. She could not help but think what might have been if Katherine and Donna had not asked her about her and Rhem's date. How would her life with him have played out? What doors might fate have opened or closed? Or had their lives been unveiled exactly as fate had intended?

Until hearing his words, she had said she did not believe in coincidences; now she was not so sure. After all, they were both single and in Green River Cove again. Was their chance encounter Fate's way of correcting the wrong, like a rubber band might snap back into place after being stretched beyond its capacity? These were the thoughts she pondered before finally drifting off to sleep.

Chapter 6

Her office chair was familiar with its thick leather seams that disappeared like a road somewhere under the seat and metal hand rests that fit the length of her arms perfectly. She had not liked its color at first, it was something akin to a cross between the color of forest and a frog. Over the years of inhabiting one of two corner offices at Leopold Media, it had grown on her, especially after she had coordinated the colors of everything else in the room around it. Once upon a time, the room and its contents were a reflection of her tastes, some learned, others acquired. She had decorated it with just the right combination of professional and personal memorabilia. But as she leaned back and surveyed the room, her eyes drifted across the perfectly placed row of framed photographs, her eyes pausing momentarily upon a more recent one she had taken with Samantha and her father. They looked happy and content, like an ordinary family. The thought was there, like a splinter in the deepest confines of her heart; what would it feel like to really be a part of a circle, again, instead of simply imitating one for the camera. And would an opportunity to connect with someone like that, ever present itself again?

Although she was not certain why, the thought of Rhem was bothersome and she pushed it away as quickly as it happened upon her. Her mind battled back and forth as she fought to pull her eyes away from the photo and push past the thoughts of Rhem, both then and now. Knowing he had not dumped her should have been comforting, but it was not. At least, not in the way it should have been. He had spent the last twenty years as hurt and angry with her as she had been with him, and it was all for nothing. Neither of them had intentionally walked away. Yet, neither had fought to hold unto the other, either.

Green River Cove seemed a world away from the fancy office at Leopold Media, with its quaint, paved walkways and warm, lighted store fronts. She felt like a voyeur, a peeping Tom, looking through the window into an open room in a house that did not belong to her. Yet it did, and its cool, sophisticated window treatments and framed artwork as a backdrop to expensive furnishings was no longer a valid representation of who she was now.

She had only been away from North Carolina a short time, but it felt longer, like a year had passed with every turn of the clock's hand while she had been in

Green River Cove. She stole another glance around the office, feeling more like a squatter than ever before. And after the first of the year, when the acquisition of Cove Bottling was behind her and Samantha's freshmen year in college was behind them, an office makeover was called for. Perhaps, something more woodsy and natural, like a rustic farmhouse, would be a better reflection of who she was now.

"They're waiting for you in the conference room." Sandra's sudden presence in the office was a welcomed distraction. Her assistant was tall and slender with long dark hair that she pulled back so that it wrapped around her dark face, like a glove. There were only a few years difference in their ages but Sandra had a amazing talent for dressing and seeming younger than she was, a trait that worked in Leopold Media's advantage, especially if the task pending was related to a work order or late delivery into or out of the dock. She was a miracle worker in a tight-fitting suit and heels.

It was instinct, the way Avery checked her watch, frantically jumped to her feet, and grabbed anxiously at the thick, heavy portfolio that lay atop the desk. Ten minutes after the hour, she checked herself in the mirror, hoping no one would notice the circles under her eyes. And if they did, they would equate it to the earliness of the hour of her flight from Kentucky instead of sleep loss deliberating the loss of an old flame, one she had not interacted with in nearly twenty years.

"You look fine," Sandra snatched the portfolio. "I told them your flight was delayed and you'd only just arrived." She pushed the fat notebook into Avery's arms and ushered her out of the office, just as she had done multiple times before. And the route from her office to the conference room was as familiar as if she were walking to a favorite coffee house or café near her home. But once she reached the end of the hallway and could see through the glass window into the conference room, it was apparent the morning was going to be business as usual, just not the state of the business she expected.

****

Even though Avery was late to the meeting, there was no urgency to initiating the meeting once she arrived, which felt like a contradiction given the urgency of the request for her attendance only a day earlier. It took several minutes for greetings to be exchanged, coffee to be acquired, and seats to be musically arranged into a particular order around the table.

Once the chairs were placed and seats taken, the room stilled to such extent, it was uncomfortable, and Avery knew she was not the only one in the room who could sense the tension. At the table's head, Matthew Leopold sat, back straight as an arrow, arms folded as if he were a defendant awaiting the verdict of a deliberating jury. He was an attractive man in an informal kind of way, with salt and pepper hair that had turned more salt than pepper since assuming his father's seat as chairman of the board several years earlier.

His popularity was hit or miss, depending on the intended outcome of his endeavor. Matthew had big shoes to fill, as his father was genuinely well-liked by the employees of Leopold Media. Abraham Leopold was a genuinely caring leader who routinely directed the company on paths that had proven benefit to both the company as well as the staff. The same could not be said of Matthew whose business decisions were usually based on his own financial benefit. His divorce, three years earlier, had done little to improve his empathy or concern for others. His immediate plan for the company was to improve his company's bottom line to the extent that at such time the company was either sold or he retired, his financial package would be more than enough to support his current lifestyle as well as that of his ex-wife and children.

"Sorry to interrupt your visit home," Matthew motioned towards Avery, but his attention did not falter from the paperwork aligned perfectly under his nose. "I trust we'll be able to get you back on the first flight out this evening." Although he had meant it as a question, it did not come out that way, especially given the lack of indecision she saw in his eyes when he finally looked up to make contact with hers.

"I trust you've managed to break away from work long enough to become reacquainted with your family and friends?" It was obvious he was not expecting a response from her or had any true interest in any level of engagement she had managed to have with her family. He was showboating for those in attendance at the meeting like a ring master on center stage at the circus and all eyes were upon him as he pranced the periphery and held the tiger at bay.

"You must be wondering why you've been summoned back," he paused as if he expected a response but went on before she could answer. "There has been a change in our strategy for the acquisition and I want to make sure you're aware and on board."

A change, she heard the word echo across the room and smack against her brain like a fist pounding upon a door. What had changed since the deal had been sealed? Before she could ask for further explanation, he cleared his throat and shuffled through the papers, weaving through the individual sheets until his fingers landed upon the document he sought.

"Has the fully executed acquisition agreement been forwarded to the state?" his gaze was fixed upon her as he waited for her to respond. She couldn't help but feel as if she were back in school and had been called upon in class for an answer.

"It has," she looked around the room hoping someone's poker face might break and offer up some evidence of whatever was going on. It was obvious she was the odd man out in the room. "For all intents and purposes, the Cove Bottling Company in Green River Cove is now a subsidiary of Leopold Media, Inc. It's simply a matter of state acknowledging the merger and assigning a new tax identification number."

"Matthew," she pushed to her feet. "What's this about? I didn't have to make this trip to give up an update. What's changed in our strategy that warrants all this secrecy?"

"After careful analysis of the financial resources that will be required of the company to modernize Cove Bottling into this century, the board has decided that the costs are too prohibitive to continue with our initial strategy." There was no remorse in his words, nothing to suggest he had any concern for the bottling company or the members of the community who relied economically on the plant. Matthew Leopold had just as well been ordering his lunch for as much consideration he had given to his action.

She knew she should respond but she could not. Her tongue had descended to the floor and was currently wrapped around her ankles so that her balance was negatively affected, and she felt herself staggering towards the hard surface of the conference table.

"What are you saying?" she asked, though she already knew what the new strategy was going to be. She knew by the way everyone in the room had looked away, suddenly unable to make eye contact. The room had become warmer, hot even, as if someone had opened a window and allowed the hot, humid air of Summer into the room, which was impossible since they were only a week away from Christmas. They were going to close the bottling plant.

****

Avery did not bother to return to her office, neither her feet nor her stomach could cooperate to make the trip. She had to get out of the Leopold building, she could not get her breath and she feared she might vomit outside of the conference room while she waited for the elevator.

In route to the airport, she texted her ex, Craig, to bow out of dinner. There would be no way to conceal what had happened, what was about to happen, or explain the role she played in the bottling company's demise. Her head was pounding, and her heart was aching, there would be no explaining once word got out that Leopold was going to close the plant, instead of expanding it into neighboring counties. The town would be devastated, burying a part of Green River Cove's history that went back nearly a hundred years. And as hard as she tried, she could not formulate a plan to impede the new direction Leopold Media had taken. She had no choice but to return the Green River Cove, share what she had learned, and pray they might forgive her one day.

****

It was still early when the plane's wheels touched down upon the runaway of the Bluegrass Airport in Lexington. There would have been more than enough time to meet for dinner once she arrived back in Green River Cove, but she was not in the mood for company or celebration. Everywhere she turned since her arrival to town, she had been met with celebration and congratulations for her role in the acquisition. It was no secret the Milbys were in a bind financially and unsure how much longer they could keep the plant open and functioning. The offer from Leopold Media had come at just the perfect time as only a select few of the community leaders were aware of how precariously the plant was hanging on. She and Leopold were being saluted as saviors within the town. She cringed considering how quickly the town's feelings would change once the truth was out in the open. It would all come out soon enough. For now, Avery was heading to the sanctuary of her parents' home and seeking refuge within the comfort of the full-size bed in the room she once called her own. Soon, that too would be little more than a memory of another time and place.

A note pinned to her bedroom door in her mother's precise handwriting explaining how there were leftovers in the refrigerator for supper that only needed to be heated and they would return home later in the night.

Just as well, Avery thought, making her way up the stairs towards her old room where the bed was calling her name. Her stomach had revolted at the consideration of food ever since Matthew had shared Leopold Media's new strategic direction. As a result, the leftovers were of no concern. As she loitered through her parents' empty house, she wanted nothing more than a long shower to wash the Leopold stench away before falling into bed.

****

Cove Bottling company had not changed much over the years since Avery had last toured the plant and enjoyed the refreshing citrus flavor of Rush soda. The glass doors of the plant entrance were the same as they had been years earlier when she was a child. Only the logo had changed with the passing of time, but up in the right-hand corner of both doors was a small, green locomotive with the Rush soda can on its barrel. It was exactly as she remembered it from the last time she had leaped its steps during its visit to Green River Cove Elementary school. She fought back the tears and wiped anxiously at those who defied her wish and fell down her cheek.

Brooke arrived only a few minutes later, firing questions about Rhem as quickly as the thought lit upon her mind. Avery was grateful for the distraction. The weight of Leopold Media's announcement foreshadowed all else, even the dramatic outcome of Avery's first love and loss. And the dark circles under her eyes were a testament to the little sleep she had gotten once she had fallen into bed. Thankfully, Brooke assumed, Avery's sleeplessness was a result of the altercation with Rhem and did not press the issue any further.

The same could not be said of Paige, once she arrived. The questions flew from her mouth as if they had been ignited from a cannon. Had Rhem reached out? Had he apologized? Didn't he understand how the miscommunication had occurred? Did Avery want a mediator? Was she okay? Did she need anything?

The relief that flooded Avery's face when Patterson Milby and his executive team showed up on the steps with keys to the plant in hand was unprecedented. But her relief was short-lived as she watched Patterson unlock the door and hold it open for the others to enter and make their way into the conference room.

The purpose of the tour, Patterson told the group, was to document any personal affects that needed to be vacated from the plant and photograph specific proposed construction areas as requested by Leopold Media. It was also the last chance for the local historian, Brendan Hall, and the Board of Commissioners to reminisce about times long since gone and commemorate the immediate time in video and pictures.

Touring the lounge and offices took very little time but once the group made their way through the twists and turns of the factory floor, the pace slowed down to a near crawl. And with good reason, it had been many years since Avery had considered the many steps in the process of bringing a can of Rush to the market. Although, once upon a time, she could have recanted all the raw ingredients required as well as the steps needed to prepare it, that was no longer the case. In took much effort to remember. She recollected water, sugar and something about carbon dioxide but could not longer recall the specifics.

Carbonating had always been her favorite step as a youngster. The pages of time flipped backwards as she reflected upon the fascination she and her friends exhibited as the bubbles danced like fireflies inside the huge bins of liquid. Once, when she was in the fourth grade, one of the workers who managed the injector had allowed several of the children, including Avery, to press the button that worked the plunger. It was one of her favorite memories of visiting the plant, even now as an adult. And the realization that those tours would now cease left a stabbing pain in the center of her chest.

"What's wrong?" Brooke brushed up against her like they had done as children when something was bothering one of them.

"Nothing," Avery lied, although past experiences told her it would be useless to lie to either of them but especially Brooke. There were seldom secrets between them and Brooke had always been able to peer through

Avery's most decisively built wall, tear down the barriers, and get to the naked truth.

"You both need a good beating," Brooke laughed. "My Momma would say, we take you both to the woodshed, tan your butts, and lock you up together until you have worked through this."

"It's not that simple," Avery tried to pull away, noting that the rest of the tour had moved on to the refrigeration and quality control. "We have to catch up, I want to watch them fashion the green, glass bottles into the finished product."

"It's too hot to go into that area. That's my least favorite part of the tour," Paige jumped in, gathering between the two of them as if they were in the school hallway and had paused at their locker. "I spoke to Rhem yesterday while you were in North Carolina and he's really hoping to work this out with you."

"It's not that," Avery pointed towards the doors that led to the loading dock and motioned for them to follow her. "I won't be in Green River Cove after the first of the year. There's no point in starting anything that we can't finish." She thought about adding how once the truth was out about Leopold Media, friendships would be tested. "Besides," she lamented as if reciting a poem, "we aren't children anymore. It would be pointless to even consider we could ever be more than old friends who went to school together once upon a time."

"Yet," Brooke moved as close against her as she could, their shoulders aligned side by side. "We know that you have, considered it, I mean."

The wind was cold against her face as Avery stepped past her and onto the receiving dock before leaning with her back against the wall looking out across the vast expanse of land behind the factory. The immediate area behind the plant was flat and the few evergreen trees visible were spread across the land like soldiers. Several hundred yards away, the dark images of the trees that made up the forest were aligned as if to indicate where the property line of the plant ended and Mr. Ridgepoint's homestead began.

During the Summer, Mr. Ridgepoint's forest grew so thick, it was as if the land was blanketed by thick, fuzzy blankets that marked the land until it disappeared into the muddy bank of the Green River. Both Confederate and Union soldiers had claimed the woods as their own during the war between the states and the land had been fertilized by the blood of those who had fallen within its creeks and ravines.

Before the soldiers had laid claim, before the English settlers made their way across the ocean, the forest had been inhabited by the Apache Indians. Various tools and other artifacts were routinely dug up in and around Green River Cove, especially in the Spring when fields were prepped for new planting. And several times over the last five years, the archaeology club at the high school was allowed a few places to excavate on various properties in the county, both public and private. Most concluded with little to no bounty but the experience left many of the students motivated towards an advanced study and no one in Green River Cove was more invested in the town's providence than Mr. Hall.

He was a common fixture at construction sites anywhere in and around Green River Cove, contracted by the Board of Indian Affairs, themselves, to supervise any disruptions of what could potentially be sacred Indian grounds and to supervise any retrieval that might be forthcoming. The last time his services had been required was during breaking of ground for the new Kroger behind the town square. After several pieces of pottery were unearthed by the bulldozer, work had ceased for over a month while the construction company waited on an approval from the Board of Indian Affairs to continue the project. He had been instrumental in mediating a resolution that met the needs of the Board of Indian Affairs and the construction company.

It had been many years since she had seen Mr. Hall and she made a mental note to seek him out before her visit came to an end.

Rhem's presence at the door behind them was both a surprise and a distraction. It was obvious he had come from working at the hotel as remnants of saw dust covered the toes of his boots and plaster board clung precariously to the locks of his hair, making him appear older against the outline of the setting sun.

"What are you doing here?" Avery's words were bolder, more confident than she felt. Inside her stomach was churning, the acid leaping up like flames to lick at her throat. She fought back the urge to vomit and hope he did not notice how watery her eyes had become and how perspiration glistened on her forehead where it met her hairline. She knew the probability of running into him again was high but if she timed her visits in and out of her parents' bookstore around his work schedule, more than likely, the Silent Night Christmas Eve festival would be their last opportunity to engage before she returned to North Carolina. And once news of Leopold Media's change of direction was made public, it might behoove her to take her exit, soon after. No one would be in the mood for a celebration, Christmas or not, and it was unlikely her participation would be welcomed.

"Sorry, I'm late," he answered over her as if he did not hear. Although it was obvious that he had. "I was waiting on Mr. Tucker to deliver a truck load of flooring," he pushed a big hand through his hair and smiled, a calming gesture she remembered from his days on the basketball court.

"Why are you here?" she asked again, less frantic this time but still not making eye contact with him. It was easier, she knew, to pretend she did not recall the fragrance of his cologne as they danced to Survivor's Eye of the Tiger, if she weren't drowning in his eyes.

"I'm the community board member," he answered as if she should have known how each county's board of commissioners required one community member to represent the interests of the town at large. When asked to represent the lay people of Green River Cove, Rhem had eagerly accepted the nomination.

"Where's everyone else?" he looked around the immediate area as if he had lost something.

"In the bottling room," Paige laughed. "That's always everyone's favorite part of the bottling tour. Watching those empty green bottles spin around on the conveyor belt and come out the other end filled with Rush soda has always been such a—" she paused.

"Rush!" Brooke and Paige answered simultaneously, laughing as if they were back in middle school and were swinging in tandem off the monkey bars.

"It was definitely my favorite part of the tour when my class came here." His grin paused as he looked toward Avery as if giving her the time to share a recollection of her own. When she did not take advantage of the consideration, he went on. "Hope I haven't missed any milestone document signing or handshake opportunity?" He brushed the hair away from his eyes and struck a pose. "Or photo op?"

"There's no media today, just us," Brooke responded reaching for her phone as its shrill resonated over their laughter. "I see," she answered to the caller. "I'll be right there."

"My assistant," she slid the phone back into her pocket and turned to face Avery. "It's Leopold Media, they've set up a conference call in thirty minutes. Probably just finalizing the last details of the transition plan?"

"I've got to get back to the store," Avery pulled her satchel as high on her shoulder as she could and wished the strap were wide enough to cover her whole face so she might disappear. No doubt, Leopold was calling to update Brooke on the acquisition change. It would all be different then; the town would be buried under a dark cloud of anger and fear. No doubt, some of the blame would be hers to bear, as an agent of Leopold Media. It would mean very little that she had been born in Green River Cove. That was a long time ago. She was an outsider, now.

Chapter 7

She did not feel much like returning to the bookstore, afterall. She did not really think of it as hiding. It was simply best to postpone the inevitable for as long as she could. The town folk would want answers once Brooke's call with Leopold Media was completed. They were less likely to invade the sanctuary of her parents' home while popping into the bookstore for a quick chat felt less intrusive.

She was surprised to find her Mom at the kitchen table, anxiously sorting through puzzle pieces and tossing the straight edges onto the rough surface of the table. On either side of her was a partially full cup of cooled coffee and a half-eaten croissant from Paige's café. Although the weather outside was cool and windy, the calm fire burning in the hearth left the room warm and toasty.

It took only a few minutes for Avery to share what would soon be common knowledge about the Cove Bottling Company deal. Patricia did not have to ask;

she knew Avery was feeling guilty about the role she had played in the acquisition and how the town might perceive her part in the merger.

"You were born here," Patricia said. "This will always be your home no matter how long you reside in North Carolina. Your roots are here, and they are buried deep."

"But Leopold—"

"You catch a plane back to North Carolina tomorrow and fight them. Draw the line and take a stand, one side or the other. You can't be in the middle."

"And if I get fired?" Avery had not really considered they might terminate her if the deal fell through, but it felt real enough once the question was out of her mouth.

"You can always come home to Green River Cove?" Patricia's eyes lit up and her body went rigid with excitement. "Your Father and I have wished that at least one of our children might be closer. And honestly, we always thought it would be you."

"Gee Mom," Avery exhaled a deep breath. It was like adding fuel to the flame, but her mother had backed right up into the discussion. "How would that work if I move back to Green River Cove just as you and Dad are selling the house and bookstore?"

"I had a feeling you knew," Patricia's posture deflated as if she had sprung a leak and the air was seeping out from a valve in her back.

"I accidently came upon the real estate contract for the house and bookstore in the drawer." Avery's face paled, a ghostly white as if an apparition had stepped into her body. "Mom," she pleaded, scooting their chairs closer together. "What's going on? Why would you and Dad sell everything and not discuss it with your children?"

"Because all three of you have independent lives and we did not want anyone to disrupt their lives in order to facilitate this new chapter for us." She pushed the box of puzzle pieces towards the middle of the table. "We want to travel while we are still in good health and able to do so."

"Travel?" Avery fought back a skeptical laugh. "Dad hates the crowds at the airport and neither of you are fond of water, so taking a cruise is out."

"No," Patricia giggled, "we put a down payment on an RV. Once we sell the house and store, we'll pay the balance and put the rest in savings. Between our IRA, savings, and social security, we can really enjoy our retirement."

"And you didn't consider selling the family home and business might, at the very least, warrant discussion with your children who also grew up in that house?"

"Little will change for any of you, dear," Patricia sounded older, wiser, as if she had been rehearsing the argument. "You and your siblings' visits home are centered around the holidays. And that won't change except we will have to gather at one of your residences or take turns."

"You should get started on that reservation back to North Carolina for tomorrow. I'm sure the word is out by now. Brooke has had more than enough time to complete her call with your company. There are no secrets anymore."

Avery checked her phone, surprised Brooke, or at the very least Paige, had not called to discuss a counter strategy. She could see them in her mind's eye, gathered at Paige's with the closed sign on the front door, outlining the pros and cons of one option over another. Avery's head hurt, with the exercise of determining which option was earmarked by her name.

The text from Brooke was simple and to the point. *Call me, we need to talk,* it read.

It would have been easier and more straightforward to simply pick up the phone and call her and try to explain exactly what had happened and how. But there was little need, Avery rationalized. After speaking with Leopold Media, Brooke would be privy to all the information as Avery knew it. Matthew had shared nothing more beyond the financial constraints of transitioning the plant versus demolishing the plant. He had elaborated on nothing beyond his new strategy and did not ask for feedback of any kind. In short, he was not asking for consent. His decision was made, he was simply disseminating the information.

Can't, Avery texted back. *Going back to NC in the AM to try and change Matthew's mind. Talk tomorrow when I return. I'm sorry.*

When did you know? Brooke's text lit up Avery's phone making it obvious she was already texting before reading Avery's last response.

Yesterday when they called me back to NC. Avery's fingers flew over the keys on her phone as if she were playing a piano. She watched and waited for another text, but it was not forthcoming. All she could do is hope Matthew would listen to reason and her plea for his reconsideration.

****

It was unusually quiet inside Paige's café, especially given the number of people who were crammed inside, as Gaylin moved dance-like from table to table, refilling coffee cups and bringing new cups for the newcomers who arrived late to the emergency meeting. She finished her last floral delivery for the day hours ago and came directly to the café as soon as she received the emergency text from the mayor's office.

Gaylin had only been a member of the chamber of commerce for a few months, but it was a role she took very seriously, especially since the appointment had come from the mayor who was one of her cousin's oldest and dearest friends. Besides, once Gaylin fully read the text, and understood the gravity of what had triggered the meeting, she knew she had to attend. Her cousin's reputation would be in question and Gaylin wanted to be there to set the record straight and protect her cousin, just as she had always done. She set the coffee pot down on the counter and rushed towards the locked door where she could make out the image of her uncle on the other side. Seemed as if she was not the only member of the family who had showed up on Avery's behalf. Ward would be in attendance as well, and no one would support or defend her more.

"Is Aunt Patricia with you?" Gaylin looked out into the darkness where the streetlights lit up the immediate area under each pole, making it look more like an elaborate game of hopscotch than the paved sidewalk along Main Street. Although most businesses were closed for the evening, some such as the diner and gas station were still open, their internal lights visible from the café's door. Other than the steady stream of patrons of those establishments, everyone else on Main Street was in route to the café for the emergency meeting.

"No," Ward pushed himself into the small opening Gaylin had left and slid out of his coat before tossing it anxiously over the coat rack against the back wall. "She's back at the house with Avery."

"How is she?" Gaylin asked, although she already knew the answer and that her cousin would, no doubt, feel responsible for what had transpired.

"She's going back to North Carolina tomorrow to try and reason with him," Ward answered, falling into the booth with two of the five commissioners.

"How long has she known?" an older man asked once Ward was seated uncomfortably close to him. "Or was this the strategy all along?"

"Say again, Juan?" Ward asked, his fists clenched atop the table. Most that knew Ward could attest he seldom had a negative word to share about anyone. He was a compassionate and genuine man who valued his family and his community.

"It can't be a coincidence they sent her to manage the acquisition. Perhaps, they knew we'd let our guard down and assume we could trust her and her company." Juan was new to Green River Cove as well as to his role within the Board of Commissioners. He lived well outside the city limits of town but owned a large car dealership on the edge of town. He was tall with lanky arms and a lean body frame, the kind that came from jogging. His hair was silver and sleek, and he wore it cropped close against his scalp. Although he was of Latin ancestry, his morning runs left his skin dark and tan as a result of the rising sun's rays.

"You can trust my cousin, Juan!" Gaylin dropped the cup loudly atop the table, it echoed across the room and caused an immediate hush. Her face was flushed and her fists were clenched as she stared him down waiting for his rebuttal.

From across the room, Paige watched Gaylin, reminiscent of the year they had all went to Paducah for 4H Summer camp. There was a boy in middle school, Avery liked. One who had not taken the same interest in her as she had him. Most of the night she waited at the other end of the roaring bonfire for him to ask her to "Sally Down the Alley" and watched as he danced with girl after girl, staking little interest in Avery.

It had been hard on Gaylin to witness the hurt and disappointment that laid upon her cousin's face. When Gaylin's turn to dance came around, she skipped to where he stood and chose him as her partner to make the trip around the fire. However, they had only gone a few paces until she pushed him into Avery's space, forcing him to take Avery around the firelit pathway, instead.

Later, after the fire was extinguished and the girls were back at the cabin, tucked two by two into the bunk beds, with Avery already sound asleep, Brooke's inquiry to Gaylin was fraught with genuine curiosity. "Why'd you do that?" She pulled the blanket as tightly under her chin as she could. "It was obvious Aidan did not want to dance with her."

"She wanted to dance with him," Gaylin explained with little indifference. "It's that simple." Some thirty years later, Gaylin had the same look upon her face as she did that night. Her cousin needed her support and she had given it, unconditionally. In an instant, it felt as if the entire room had been transported by a wormhole or other vortex back to that Summer. In their mind's eye, they watched the interaction between the cousins for what was perceived as a "threat." And the room grew silent for the moment as if paying the recollection its due respect. It was not long, however, before the silence was broken.

"Then where is she?" Juan waved his arms around the room. "Why isn't she here with us, trying to mitigate the damage?"

"She's going back to Leopold Media in the morning and try to reason with him," Ward mentioned, monitoring the temperature of the room. Crowds could be tricky and there was a fine line between a gathering and a mob.

"Besides," Brooke chimed in, "I've been managing the acquisition, Juan, not Avery." Her eyes narrowed. "So if there's a question of how the project's been managed from our end, let's hear it now."

"What exactly has happened?" the farmer, Mr. Minor, asked, pulling at his suspenders as if they were his lifeline, holding him up in his seat. "I've heard from a lot of people in this room." He eyes the room like he was in a gunfight before continuing. "I'd like to hear the actual facts from either Patterson Milby or the town's legal counsel."

Patterson Milby straightened his expensive, silk tie and walked to the center of the café and motioned for Brooke to join him in addressing the crowd. "When we were initially approached by Leopold Media about acquiring Cove Bottling company, the agreement we entered into was one of growth and expansion using the existing network accessible to Leopold to distribute Rush soda outside the geographical local counties."

He cleared his throat and motioned to Paige that he would like a glass of water before going on. "Our overall partnership goals were to keep the history and charm of the existing bottling company currently here in Green River Cove and expand in phases as far North as Michigan, as far East as New York, and down South into Georgia." He paused to let the audience absorb the demographics he shared. "In phase two, we would distribute into the four corners of the US, including Florida, the New England States, and California."

"We've been working on the deal for the better part of a year," Brooke added, moving to stand slightly in front of Patterson, "and were ecstatic last week when we put pen to paper."

"This growth associated with this agreement would have brought hundreds of new jobs to Green River Cove and put us on the map for food services distribution. It was supposed to be a new life for Rush soda and for us." Patterson paused, sounding more like the Pastor at the big Christian church in town. "Most of you are aware, my family has been struggling to keep the doors open and jobs within the community. It broke my family's heart to have to issue those layoffs last year, but we had no choice. It was the only way to save the company."

"And when Leopold Media approached us," Brooke summarized, "we knew it was the best path for the company and a Godsend for the town."

"How much is the acquisition worth?" Juan spat out as if he were bidding on an item at auction.

"The financial language and terms of the agreement are confidential," Brooke explained against the roar of the crowd who saw her response as part of the conspiracy.

"The executives have a vested interest in keeping the acquisition costs at or below those mentioned in the agreement?" Juan added, eyeing Ward across the table as if they were cowboys ready to dual.

"Again," Brooke responded through clenched teeth, "any financial language in the agreement cannot be discussed by any member of the executive team related to the buyer or seller."

"You just answered the question," Juan barked. The crowd rumbled again, its cadence growing rapidly like that of a beating heart. He struggled to make his way from the booth, his boots heavy upon the café floor. "This was probably the plan all along, we've been duped by a life-sized board game full of smoke and mirrors."

"Juan," Paige warned, slamming the ceramic coffee pot against the counter with such force, the container burst into dozens of pieces as thick, dark, coffee spilled over the broken pieces and onto the floor. "You aren't from here so I will forgive your trespass, but that's NOT how we operate." She stepped from behind the counter with apologetic tears in her eyes as one of the servers wiped at the mess on the counter and floor. "The Milby family has worked tirelessly for years to ensure the factory flourishes for many years to come. Many of us in the room have grown up within the walls of that factory and with a bottle of Rush in our hand."

She moved so close into his space that he was forced to take a step back as she went on as if he were the only person in the room. "All of us who grew up here would do anything within our power to keep the factory open. All of us," she repeated, "including those who live in Green River Cove and those who have moved away, have a heartfelt interest in its success." Paige wiped at the tears that fell freely down her cheeks and inhaled a healthy breath. "We are meeting here tonight to propose solutions, not point fingers." Her pace was brisk as she walked to the door and pulled it open, trying not to flinch as the cool air rushed into the room. "Anyone who came to point fingers should leave now. Your input isn't needed tonight." She watched with baited-breath as the crowd settled and Juan retook his seat in the booth.

She was not sure at what point during the discussion Rhem had arrived as she had not seen him enter the café or take a seat. However, it was impossible not to notice him since he towered over most everyone else aligned along the back wall of the café. What was most noticeable, however, was the skeptical expression on his face as the group's chatter became less audible and more like the roar of a speeding train.

Paige exchanged a worried glance with Brooke, hoping Brooke might read her body language like when they were in school. Juan was a nut case, everyone knew that. But Rhem, he was one of them. He was born in Green River Cove, he knew Avery, knew she would never willingly perpetuate any action that would negatively affect the town or its people. It would have been like putting a gun to her own head. He must know that, didn't he?

Chapter 8

The trip back to North Carolina had been a waste. Matthew Leopold had not even bothered to convene any of the Board of Directors. He was the only person in attendance and made it clear before she had even taken her seat that he had only allotted ten minutes for her to plead her case.

And plead she did. In fact, she had borderline begged him to reconsider and not shut down the plant. He had much to consider during the twenty-four hours since making the announcement. Leopold Media's new strategy involved not only shutting down the plant but dismantling it to sell as for scrap. Apparently, the return on the investment for the resale of warehouse and office equipment was substantial and would increase Leopold's bottom line.

The land, he gloated, had been the best part of the agreement as it was located near enough to the railroad tracks to make an ideal distribution center for Leopold

Media's established portfolio of products. Once the building was leveled, the land would be cleared and made ready for the new buildings that would become Leopold Media Distribution by this time next year.

"Was this the plan all along?" She fought to keep her voice steady; all she wanted to do was cry but she would not give him the satisfaction. She pushed herself to her feet, feeling small seated in the chair across from him. "I brought Cove to you in good faith and my plan was solid. It will make you money over the long term."

"It will," he rubbed the tips of his fingers as one might assess a new manicure. "But tearing it down and putting a new distribution center there for products we produce that are already successful will make five times that amount in less than two years." His smile was ingenuine as he added, "Your bonus and dividends from this deal alone will make you a rich young woman."

"I don't care about the money," she wanted to smack him. This was her town, her family, and friends he had assigned a monetary value to. He had reduced their livelihood to little more than things and assets. And she hated him for it.

"Come now," his words were arrogant. "Everyone cares about money."

"I don't," she grabbed her jacket from the back of the chair and took her exit, making sure to leave the door hanging wide open as she hurled herself through it. Hopefully, there would be a taxi waiting outside; she had to get to the airport and back to Green River Cove as soon as was possible. There had to be a way to stop him, and she would stop at nothing to find it.

****

She should have skipped supper and went straight to her parents' home once her flight from North Carolina landed at the airport in Lexington, but she did not. True, the rumbling of her stomach had grown more persistent since the muffin and coffee she had devoured prior to getting on the airplane. But mostly, she was tired of avoiding everyone. The sooner she faced the townspeople of Green River Cove, the sooner the healing could begin. And regeneration could not start until the band-aid was ripped away.

Avery asked the server for a table in the back of the diner where the lights were not as bright, and she might consume her meal in private before the tribunal began. Once she was seated, she texted her parents, as well as Brooke and Paige, to let them know she was home and was having a bite at the diner. In was not that Avery minded eating alone, it was not an uncommon event since the divorce, and Samantha was away at college. The long hours associated with being on the executive leadership team at work left little time for a social life. It was more convenient to detour at a local restaurant for a sandwich or salad on her way home from the office than to cook for one upon arriving at home.

It was, however, an isolated event to dine alone within the township of Green River Cove. Try as she might, she could not recollect ever engaging in such activity. And the curious stares and side glances from several of the other customers while she waited for the server to take her order, made the incident even more awkward. She felt like a celebrity and not in a good way.

"Whatcha having tonight sweetie?" the server asked before her orthopedic shoes had even come to a full stop at the table. "The usual?"

Avery paused, considering if the older woman had mistaken her for someone else or really recollected the many years earlier when Avery routinely ordered a grilled cheese sandwich with white bread and American cheese with a side order of fries. Her heart ached at the thought of the time that had passed, seeing the hand on the clock spin in double time. Some of the years had been harder than others as evident by the salting of her hair. Did Gloria see the image of a young Avery and her friends poured into the booth looking upon her or was the image, mature and aged?

"What's my usual, Gloria?" Avery bit her lip, needing to belong once again in Green River Cove, so badly, she feared she might cry if Gloria did not know what her usual order would be.

"American cheese on white bread and fries," Gloria did not look up. Instead, she scribbled on the pad and moved to another table where a couple was just about to sit. "You want a Rush with that?"

"I do," Avery breathed a sigh of relief, "from the bottle though, not on tap."

"Better get a few for the road," an unfamiliar voice advised from the bar. "I hear they'll be hard to come by, pretty soon." There was chatter from the counter as several others offered commentary that was lost in translation.

She wanted to turn around and determine if the man was someone she knew. More than likely, he was not known to her. Anyone she knew would have wanted to have the discussion in private.

"Course," the man went on, raising his voice so that he could be better heard over the noise of the rumble of conversations at the counter. "Once they close the plant, you'll be gone again and won't give it a moment's thought."

"Gloria," Avery caught the server gently by the arm. "Could you make my order to go, please?"

"Don't do that," Rhem appeared into the dim light like a ghost and slid into the chair across the table from her. "Stay, I want to talk to you." He spoke tenderly to both Avery and the server. "I'll have the same as her, please."

"You don't have to do this," Avery's hand moved to collect her satchel. She no longer had an appetite. She should just cancel the order altogether and leave. No doubt, she could make a sandwich or something at her parents' house once her stomach's rumbling resumed.

"I'm sorry," he leaned across the table so close to her, she caught a scent of his shampoo. "I owe you an apology." He reached for her hand, but she pulled it away before he could make contact. "I eavesdropped on a private conversation and misinterpreted what I heard."

"We've been through this already. It was a long time ago and we both were at fault. I should have sought you out and asked you to your face why you no longer wanted to hang out with me."

"And I should have asked you about what I overheard, instead of shutting you out," he reached for her hand, waiting patiently for her to take it.

She slipped her hand into his and breathed a sigh of relief. After so many years of wondering and lamenting over what might have been or what could have been, her thoughts were centered and out in the open. It was a good feeling, and she knew by the way he looked at her across the table, he felt the same way.

"Gloria?" Juan called from the counter, "ready for the check when you get a minute." He exchanged a glance with several of the customers at the bar. "Remember to give me my senior citizen's discount; be needing every penny once we close the bottling company."

It was not clear if he was alone at the diner or with one or more of those seated around him. But the chatter that was prominent earlier had diminished. Only Juan's taunting was as evident.

Gloria made her way towards him, and by her pace, she was anxious to have him pay up and get out. However, Rhem rose to his feet and intercepted before she reached her destination, reaching tenderly for the bill intended for Juan.

"This one's on me, Juan." Rhem folded the bill and stuffed it into his shirt pocket.

Juan was obviously embarrassed, his face flushed red and clearly visible even in the dim light of the diner. "I can afford to pay for my dinner, son." He slid off the stool, his hand fumbling in his back pocket for the wallet he kept there.

"It's my pleasure," Rhem smiled. "Just subtract this amount from the pennies you'll be needing in the event the bottling plant is forced to close."

"I'm just looking out for the town, Rhem," Juan's tongue tripped over his bottom lip.

"Everyone is concerned, Juan," Rhem explained, looking to Juan but speaking at the others gathered around him. "Will the town struggle if the bottling company closes? Of course we will, but we will get through it in the same way we have faced all the obstacles in this town's history. We will face it together."

Rhem turned to face Avery. "We support one another here." His eyes drifted back to Juan. "And we never turn on one another. Never!"

"He's right!" Everyone's eyes went to the diner's entrance where Paige and Brooke waited, coats draped over their arms as if they had just come from someplace else. Paige stepped further into the room and went on. "Regardless of what happens with Cove Bottling, we have to put our heads together and come up with other options."

Avery felt the warm hand of her friend on her shoulder, as Brooke came to stand by the table. "We aren't defeated yet, folks," she added. "We are all working around the clock to figure something out." She took the seat next to Avery as Rhem returned to his seat and Paige plopped into the remaining chair.

"Do we really have options?" Avery asked, once Juan had left and the others returned to the task of having their evening meal. "Or was that just to defuse the situation?"

"Juan Soto is acting like a jerk," Paige added. "He's not usually like this; I've never seen him so self-absorbed."

"He's scared," Avery explained. "Everyone is, he's just being more obvious about it."

"I see you two have worked things out?" Paige shared a knowing glance with Avery and Rhem before her eyes fell on the two plates of food that Gloria had placed on the table during the altercation with Juan. She snatched a french fry from one of the plates and popped it into her mouth before folding her arms across her chest in deliberation.

"Let's just say," Rhem smiled to Avery across the table as if answering for them both, "that we've opted to move on and start anew."

"I think that sounds like a good plan," Brooke agreed, reaching for half of his sandwich. "I don't think I have had grilled cheese and fries since the last time we were all here together."

"Old habits," Avery pushed her plate towards Paige indicating she should help herself to the other half of sandwich still on the plate.

"Die never," Paige laughed, pushing the end of the sandwich into her mouth and groaning with delight at the warm, rich, buttery taste of the grilled bread and melted cheese.

"What did Leopold say when you met with him this morning?" Brooke asked, her eyes wishful that Avery's update would be different than the last conversation she had had with the man and his executive team.

"His stance is the same," Avery explained, motioning to Gloria that their glasses needed refilling. "He made no concessions. Leopold Media will assume ownership after the first of the year. And at that time, will initiate processes to close the business and demolish the plant."

She ate the last few fries on the plate before adding, "he has a fully executed agreement and has no intention of letting us out of it."

"Maybe we could buy it back at a fair profit, of course to Leopold?" Rhem asked, his face optimistic and contorted in a way that made him look younger.

"Patterson Milby and his family could barely make the mortgage payments as they were; there's no way they could buy it back at any profit, regardless of how small," Brooke said. "And something tells me that Leopold wouldn't accept a small profit."

"She's right," Avery explained. She had been with Leopold Media for enough years to know what the targeted range was for the minimum return on any investment. As a member of the executive team, acquisitions had to yield a minimum return. And breaking the Cove Bottling deal would be an action in direct contradiction to the company's strategic mission.

"I think," Rhem took Avery's hand again, "we need a break from all this. Christmas is next week, and I've not purchased even one single gift." His eyes danced in the light as they lit upon Avery. "Any volunteers to help a guy out tomorrow?"

"I'm working," Paige answered quickly, too quickly. "I am the Mayor, you know?"

"And I've got cases scheduled in court most of the day," Brooke smiled, looking across the table to Paige.

"I've got some time," Avery smiled. "My workload seems to have been lightened."

"Perfect, I'll meet you for breakfast at Paige's and we'll go from there?" Rhem dropped Juan's bill on top of the one Gloria left at their table along with a handful of bills. The scratching of his chair across the wooden floor was a distraction. So much so, she did not realize he had kissed her cheek until she felt the warmth of his lips against her skin.

He scurried off before she could respond or react to his kiss, which was probably a good thing as she was unsure what she might have said. She had no words to describe what she was feeling, which was an oddity since she was a writer, or used to be one.

****

Christmas was alive and well along Green River Cove's Main Street, with its garland draped lampposts and holly branch centerpieces peeking out from glass domes at the top of the posts. Store windows were costumed with faux snow-covered tree skirts staged under immaculate artificial trees adorned with ornaments of every shape, size, and color. Silver and garland hung like banners from one branch to another while lights twinkled in synchronized rhythm with Christmas carols that were audible through the thick panes of glass. There were presents wrapped in glorious colors with ribbons tied into bows that overshadowed the gift to the extreme.

Other businesses, like the diner and café, displayed artistic scenes of snowmen and trees, courtesy of local artisans and schools, penciled and painted upon the glass windows with cursive holiday greetings of red and green. Aligned along the walkway and atop every exterior surface, poinsettias with long, red leaves stood proudly, some in thick holiday pots, others anchored into the plant beds once occupied by summer annuals.

The fragrance of baked goods, drippy with sugary icing, mixed with the cool December air, and was intoxicating as she and Rhem wandered past, arms laden with wrapped gifts and holiday bags but they fought the urge and wandered towards the café instead.

Even with gloves, her hands were chilled. She wanted nothing more than to hold them, ungloved over a steaming cup of hot chocolate. And if one of Paige's chocolate croissants happen to fall upon her plate, she would enjoy that too.

Rhem had been attentive, wandering in and around behind the counters at the drug store where she shopped for her mother's favorite cologne and the hardware store where the cordless drill she had ordered for her father was ready for pick up. Check by check, she marked off purchases for the rest of her family as well as Brooke and Paige, not acknowledging the lateness of the hour until Rhem mentioned he could not hear the Christmas music bellowing from the speaker hanging over the drug store entrance over the grumbling of his stomach.

Pizza, he suggested, pointing towards the drug store's entrance, and pulling her by the arm towards the door. It would be like old times, having a few slices together and sharing a pitcher of Rush on tap. How could she refuse his offer? And the kiss he planted on her lips as he pulled her into his arms and pushed them both across the threshold of the door was the tree topper on the tree. His kiss was perfect, just like she knew it would be.

****

The rest of the week was little more than a blur between prepping for the Silent Night Celebration and completing purchases of the few items that remained on the list, there was little time for much else. She spent a few hours each day helping out her parents in the store and assisting Paige with the last of the volunteer duties for Christmas Eve. She and Rhem met every evening, sometimes for dinner, other times there was only enough time for coffee and dessert.

His crew was working nonstop to ready the first floor of the hotel for open house during the celebration on Main Street. The lobby and event room would be open to the public and she could not wait to see what he had done with the place. It was like waiting to open the largest gift under the tree.

One more attempt, she told him, seated comfortably at a table at the country club lodge as close to the fireplace as was safe. Her steak was pure perfection, well-cooked in a sauce that brought out the smoky flavor of cooking over an open flame. She was not routinely a fan of asparagus, steamed, grilled, or otherwise but whatever secret the chef had for cooking it, it was amazing.

She tipped her wine glass to him, leaning as close into the center as she could and hoping he would take the hint. His kiss, like the steak, was perfection and she wished the night did not have to end. But it did, as she had—in a final attempt to reason with Matthew Leopold—booked a 7am flight back to North Carolina, meaning she needed to head for the airport around 5 in the morning. It would be a long day tomorrow and she wanted to face him and her colleagues with a good night's sleep and a fresh outlook. And she was going to pray, pray Matthew Leopold would change his mind and leave Cove Bottling to the people of Green River Cove.

Chapter 9

Matthew Leopold was not pleased to see her on his itinerary for the day and he made no qualm about expressing his unhappiness. She felt more like a high school student being reprimanded by the principal, instead of a corner office executive meeting with its CEO.

What are you thinking, he had asked her at least four times during the fifteen minutes he had allotted to their meeting. At least twice, he had questioned her loyalties, citing how she, as an employee of Leopold Media, should be celebrating the financial impact to the company as a result of the Cove Bottling company. Instead, his fists were clenched atop the desk, as if controlling his anger was all consuming. The already twisted and bent straw crumbled into pieces as he suggested her time in Green River Cove should be shortened and she might return to North Carolina and resume her duties. A distraction, he went on, being in

Green River Cove was prohibiting her from performing her responsibilities without bias and prejudice.

"Are you unapproving my vacation?" she asked, lurching from the chair as if an electric charge had passed through it.

"No," his head held onto hers. "I'm suggesting you return to North Carolina and work in the office during the week between Christmas and New Year's. I think it will be easier for you to accept if you are not there to watch the bulldozers move in and the demolition begin."

"Renovations weren't scheduled until the first week in February!" Her mind was spinning. They had even less time than they realized. The execution was approved, and the clock was nearing midnight.

"Yes," he bit his lip. "But we're waiting on suppliers for equipment and devices, now. It's a demolition and that action can be moved up."

"You're starting the week of New Year's?" She tried not to cry, there was no way they could raise enough money to seduce Matthew into selling the bottling company back.

"Actually, the area immediately behind the plant will see activity on Monday. The bulldozers and crew should arrive on site over the weekend." He checked his watch, but she knew it was not because he wanted to know the time. He was reemphasizing the extent to which she was wasting his time.

"But that's the week of Christmas Eve!" her words were louder than she intended and by his reaction, he thought so too. "We've never started a project like this on Christmas Eve before."

Before he could respond, she went on. "I've worked with you on hundreds of acquisitions. This isn't the way we do them. We've always conducted them softer, gentler, never like this. Why are you doing this?"

"My father is retiring at the end of the year," he looked away from her. "He thinks I'm soft, a bleeding heart," he all but laughed. "I have to do this to demonstrate that I have the heart to do what has to be done." He swallowed, "I'm sorry. I wish there was another way but there isn't."

He moved from behind his desk and wandered across the room to the window that overlooked the city below and pushed his hands in his front pockets. "I think he's testing me," he whispered with his back still to her. "I'm sorry, I really am, but I've no choice. It's the only way he'll appoint me into the position."

He sighed, "You're a good person, Avery. I know you don't deserve this but I've no choice."

"You're a good man, Matthew," she moved closer to him but still kept a fair distance away. "There must be another way?"

"There's not," he finally turned to face her. "But I do think it's better if you return to your office and work from here till after it's demolished." He turned back to face the window. "Take the weekend, but be in your office on Monday morning."

When he finally did spin his body back towards the door, she was gone, and the door was ajar. If not for the faint odor of her cologne, he might have thought she was a ghost, and he feared a haunting might be in his future.

****

The flight from North Carolina to Lexington was one she had taken more times than she could count and for the most part was predictable. There had been times, over the years, when the flight departed and arrived on schedule, without a hitch. Yet, other times the trip was hindered by delay after delay to the extent that she might just as easily have made the trip by car. This trip, however, did not seem to fit into either of those categories.

On one hand, she was anxious to return to Green River Cove and give her update, ineffective as it had been. On the other, she hated to share what she had learned. The demolition was slated to start the week of Christmas, what a horrible memory that would be for the community. And she hated herself for the role she had played in the tragedy.

When she made the call to have Brooke, Paige, and Rhem meet her at the hotel where they could speak in private, it had seemed like a good and efficient idea. But once they were all inside and Rhem locked the door behind them, she felt like maybe one on one would have been a better route. Even though these were her oldest and closest friends, she felt as if she was outnumbered. It took less than ten minutes to update them all and by the look on their faces, they were as shocked as she had been upon hearing the news.

Rhem was the first to speak and his question was directed specifically at Brooke. How long would it take to prepare a counteroffer to reacquire the bottling company? And how were they going to begin to raise the money?

Even if she worked through the weekend, Brooke explained, she would not be able to complete such a proposal. And any potential agreement would require the approval of the Board of Commissioners before she could present it to Leopold's legal representation. Paige agreed and reminded them, the board would not approve any agreement until they were assured proper funding was in place to support the terms of the agreement.

To further complicate their predicament, Patterson Milby and his family had utilized a portion of the acquisition funds to settle some outstanding debts. Regrettably, they no longer even had the initial amount indicated on the bill of sale. By all accounts, they were swimming against the current and eventually, the ship was going to sink. It was simply a matter of time.

****

Her father had always been a man of few words. Even when he was angry, which was not often, he had little to say. Patricia had always been easier to read, happy or sad. The details were etched upon her face like a drawing.

They were alone, the three of them, gathered behind the bookstore counter as if they were planning mutiny on the management. Thankfully, the store was empty, which was not unusual as the clock hands neared the lunch hour and the employees that worked on and around Main Street rushed in and out of the cafés and diners for a bite to eat or a coffee to go.

Luckily, Avery and her parents were able to put the private time to good use, especially with the upcoming sale of the family homestead and business. And her parents had other questions as well, about the new, old development with Rhem as well as her future with Leopold Media.

Accepting that her parents no longer had a desire to reside in the house she and her siblings had grown up in or run the family business was not going to be an easy discussion to have, but it was a topic that had to transpire. And now that Rhem was in her life again, how long could the distance between be minimized? Finally, there was her work. With all that transpired over the last week with Leopold Media, was this still where she wanted to hang her hat?

With so much focus on the community and the bottling company, it was apparent, she had given little thought to anything else. And the time had come to do just that.

****

Brooke leaned back, letting her body relax against the thick cushion of her chair, glad she had indulged and purchased an expensive desk chair for her office. It was early, too early to be in the office already, but Avery's pleading call before sunrise had prompted her to slide gently out of bed and dress by the light of the moon. There was no need to awaken her sleeping husband who had worked a double at the hospital.

If her friend had called at that hour citing the need to have a bone set or a cut sutured, she would have summoned Graham and passed the task on to him. But that was not the case. Avery had asked her to prepare something to send to Leopold Media that had to arrive before Monday morning. Matthew Leopold was expecting Avery to be in her office by 8am and she had no intention of abiding by that demand. Instead, she was sending her resignation and she wanted Brooke to draft it as soon as was possible.

"You're lucky to have a copy of your contract so readily available," Brooke said over the paper she held at eye level. The glasses that sat precariously on the tip of her nose made her look more like her mother than she probably realized. Avery wanted to share a memory of Brooke's mother that came to mind. Her mother, Rachel, worked for the county and was often the representative in the driver's license office during renewals. Often, she took the new photo for the license and destroyed the old one. There was a big box of tiny photos in her office, under the desk, that the girls loved to pilfer through, picking out pictures if it was someone they knew. But Brooke was enthralled in reviewing Avery's employee contract and probably would not appreciate the interruption.

"I wasn't planning on leaving Leopold when I arrived here," Avery paused to gather her thoughts. "Craig forwarded it to me from the joint electronic files we still share. Our wills, etc. are all easily accessible to each other in the event there's an emergency."

"Are you sure you've thought this through?" Brooke laid the paper atop the others and aligned them perfectly one atop the other. "You're angry. Maybe we should hold off on offering your resignation until after Christmas?"

"For the first time since the strategy changed, I'm thinking with clarity. I have a good reputation in this business and will have no trouble getting another job, if that's what I want." And she meant it, the change in Matthew's plan had gnawed at her like a thorn since he had acknowledged it. Her words to him were true, her company was not known in the business to be a ruthless one. And she was not going to be comfortable working for one that was. Based on what he had said, the company was changing. Maybe it was time for a change for her as well. After all, once she resigned, there would be no need to rush back to North Carolina. She could stay in Green River Cove for as long as she wanted. With Samantha attending the University of Kentucky, it would certainly enable them both to visit more frequently than if the house in North Carolina was occupied.

"So, what do we want?" Brooke retrieved the document and studied it again.

"My employment package is lucrative," Avery smiled. "I had a very efficient and capable lawyer draft it."

"Yes, you did," Brooke eyed her momentarily over the paper.

"This deal with Cove, I want them to pay me my bonus for my role in the acquisition of Cove and I want the dividends I'd be due, paid out in full, instead of over multiple years."

"How many years?" Brooke pushed her glasses higher on her nose before scribbling onto a pad nearby.

"I'm relatively young in the business world. I planned to work at least another twenty-five years. I'll settle for twenty." She watched as Brooke punched numbers into a desk calculator and assessed the number.

"That's a lot of money," she tossed her glasses atop the table and rubbed her eyes.

"Like Matthew said yesterday, I'll be a very rich woman."

"I'll get it drafted and notarized." She spun around to where the sun was just peeking above the horizon. "I still have a valid power of attorney for you. You want me to sign, or you want to?"

"You can," Avery slid into her coat.

"What are you giving them in exchange?" Brooke spun the chair around and walked to where Avery had stopped at the door. "They aren't going to just write you a check and pack up your office for you."

"I'll go quietly and sign a nondisclosure agreement for any project I've worked on for the last year, including Cove. Even though he hasn't played all of his cards, Matthew will not want to be publicly scrutinized by the court of public opinion. Although, he won't admit it, he knows what he is doing is wrong. The Board of Directors will not want to go through a public trial of Leopold Media's morality, or lack thereof."

They met at the doorway and exchanged a brief hug before pulling away from one another. It was Brooke who broke the silence. "Are you sure you're thinking with your head and not with your heart?" She opened the door for Avery to exit. "Even if you use your severance package, the bulldozers will be here on Monday."

"I know," Avery stepped through the door, "but if they agree to the terms of the severance settlement, we'll be one step closer to getting what we need to stop the demolition. Maybe we can still save some of it?"

"And we may not get to save any of it. You have to prepare yourself for that eventuality. It won't be your fault, and no one will blame you."

"Some already do," she shrugged. "I gotta go. Let me know what they say?"

"Of course," Brooke waited until Avery disappeared down the hallway and out of the door before returning to her desk and turning her attention back to Avery's employment contract. If her friend's plan worked, it would be a miracle. And that's exactly what the town needed, a Christmas miracle.

****

Avery tried to focus her thoughts as best she could. There was still no word from Matthew or anyone else at Leopold Media, although they had acknowledged her letter of resignation. Her assistant, former assistant, was instrumental in clearing out the corner office Avery previously occupied and dropping it off to Craig's office in North Carolina.

Samantha would have finished her last class before Christmas break and no doubt, be on her way from college. The trip would take her a little more than an hour, even with the university traffic out of Lexington. The clocked ticked away, each minute hand trailing behind as if it were an hour instead of a minute around the face of the clock. Her daughter had been home over the Thanksgiving holiday. Yet, it felt as if it had been many months since she had seen her. She could not wait.

The weekend seemed to drag on, yet no one in Green River Cove was anxious for its conclusion, knowing that Leopold would have the bulldozers onsite behind the plant at sunrise on Monday morning. Samantha's arrival, Friday night, left the family jovial and celebratory. But after dinner, when she left to meet up with local friends, thoughts of Monday morning returned, and the anxiety level was as thick as the fog that covered the muddy banks of the Green River in the Summer.

Paige scheduled multiple events on Saturday, tasks that required completion prior to the Silent Night Celebration and would surely keep everyone's thoughts off the inevitable events of Monday. It did not help that Leopold's crew arrived in Green River Cove late Saturday night with multiple trucks loaded with the construction crew, several vans of tools, and a trailer loaded with a full-size bulldozer. Although their hotel was just outside of town, their presence was felt as intensely as if they had parked on the lawn of the old church that stood in the middle of Main Street.

A confidential email that landed in Brooke's email late Saturday night confirmed what Avery had proposed. The Board of Directors at Leopold Media did not want a messy court battle or to have the details of any of their more prominent projects disclosed. Once Avery signed the nondisclosure agreement and the severance agreement was executed, a certified check for her would be delivered to Brooke's office. Avery knew a celebration was in order, but she also knew none would be forthcoming.

****

Thirty days, per the terms of the agreement—the plant itself would begin its shutdown in thirty days. Until then, the lines continued on schedule and staff reported to work for their assigned shifts. Vendors delivered raw materials and tractor trailers left the loading dock filled with pallets of Rush soda. It was business as usual, if not for the line of yellow LMI trucks and vans that stood out like sore thumbs against the gray landscape behind the plant. Off in the distance, the long trailer carrying the bulldozer had made the trip as far into the woods as it could. It was parked, just off the dirt road that ran from the river to the Ridgepoint farm.

No one from the leadership team at Leopold Media had made the trip to Green River Cove. Instead, the crew foreman seemed to be acting on their behalf. His name was Arnett Pauley, and given his size, it was a miracle he was able to fit into the cab of the bulldozer. He stood well over six feet tall with thick arms and legs. His chest was bloated like a puffer fish and his neck looked like the stump of a tree, which was fortunate due to the size of his head. He was a mountain with blonde crew cut hair, stuffed into a flannel shirt and cheap denim jeans.

The ground under his feet crunched as he made his way to where Paige and Brooke waited at the entrance to the bottling company with most of the Patterson family in attendance. He took his time shaking hands with each one, making sure he had everyone's cell phone number, and giving them his in return. His attention turned to Avery, who was waiting off to the side, and politely asked for her name and her purpose in being there.

He recognized her name, she knew by the way he arched his eyebrows and squinted his blue eyes. "Is there anything I need to know before we get started?"

"You'd need to check with one of the others. I'm not there in any capacity other than personal."

He turned to the others as she added, "However, we are hoping for a stay of execution?"

"I'm aware, Ma'am," he smiled a genuine smile, revealing a perfect row of white teeth. "My orders are to proceed as planned unless something in an official capacity or someone from Leopold says otherwise." He tipped his hat. "Sorry, Ma'am."

"But," he smiled, "where we initiate the digging is up to me. And I'm starting way back there towards the river." He leaned in as if he wanted to tell her a joke. "I grew up in a small town just like this. If it was me, I'd me doing exactly what you folks are."

"Thank you, Mr. Pauley," she said, smiling warmly to him.

"Arnett," he corrected her, "but I have no more control over anything else than that."

"Understood," Paige stepped closer so that she could better be a part of the discussion. "And thank you."

"My crew takes a lunch break and two ten-minute breaks every day, timed at my discretion," he slid a clipboard under his arm. "We stop when I see something I think is unsafe for them or someone with a badge tells me to."

"Got it," Avery nodded. "Thank you."

"Good luck," he walked away, looking like the lumberjack from the Brawny commercial on TV.

"We're going to need it," the group seemed to chant all at once.

"We should get going," Paige zipped her jacket as tight against her chin as she could. "Christmas Eve is Thursday. We have a lot to do for the Silent Night Celebration and there's not much we can do here until Leopold Media responds to our proposal to repurchase the plant."

"Thanks to Avery, we've got what we need to reacquire it, depending on how much he marks it up," Patterson adjusted his tie. "I'll be in my office in anyone needs me.

"And me in mine," Brooke added, grabbing her satchel from the floor of the back observation deck where they could see the yellow trucks and vans moving away from the fence, presumably to start working at a point further way from the plant, instead of right at the fence.

"I've got a meeting with the Board in an hour, if anyone is free for lunch, come to the café around one." She slid into a thick, gray parka with a fur-lined hood and waddled away looking like the Pillsbury Doughboy.

Avery took a final look towards the trucks, wishing she had paid more attention to the schematics so she would have a better idea of what was happening beyond the fence where she could not see. Were they simply dozing down the trees and landscape or were trenches and drains being placed as well? Would it take hours or days to reach the back of the deck in back? Although there was a certain comfort in not knowing when the destruction might begin, there was also solace in being ignorant of how much time they had left. She could not decide which perspective would illicit the least amount of pain and produce less of an ache. There was bliss and there was action; she was not sure if there was a difference anymore.

Chapter 10

Rhem was both surprised and happy to see her. Albeit at first she thought she might have made a mistake as his expression was anxious upon seeing her at the door of the hotel. He detoured from his work behind the counter and pulled the door to the small room closed before meeting her just inside the lobby. His kiss was warm, sweaty even, and she felt guilty for interrupting his work. He was determined to have the first floor ready for open house during the Silent Night Celebration. He had not calculated the time he was with her or helping with Cove into the time required to finish. As a result, he was behind schedule and working far beyond that of his crew to finish.

"What a nice surprise," he kissed her again, rubbing his hands up and down her arms as if he was attempting to generate some body heat. "What do I owe the pleasure?"

"Just left Cove," she looked away. "The LMI crew is here, bulldozer and all."

"I'm sorry, I know you were hoping for a different outcome," he pulled her into his arms.

"I'm not giving up yet," she mumbled into his chest. "The building is still standing," she pulled away. "I don't want to keep you from your work."

"You aren't, and I appreciate the visit," his attention turned towards the door as her father pulled himself and two large five-gallon containers through the door."

"Dad?" she rushed to help him with one of the containers. "What are you doing?"

"Bookstore is slow," he pointed his thumb next door. "Mom's able to manage on her own; thought I'd help out Rhem, here, with some painting."

"Appreciate it, Ward, I already taped off the baseboards like you asked." Rhem waved towards the counter. "I got the mail cabinet up on the wall and taped the sides off already."

"I'll let you two get to your painting," she kissed Rhem and waved to her father, "Bye, Dad, see you at home."

"Bye, honey," she heard his voice from behind the wall. "See you at home."

She was not sure if she should be surprised or not. Afterall, the bookstore was next to the hotel. No doubt, Rhem had become friendly with her parents even before her relationship with him was resumed. They were neighbors, afterall. Why then, she smiled in spite of herself, did the thought of them being friends and helping each other leave her with such a warm feeling in her stomach? It was as if fate had righted a wrong and put her life back in the order it was meant to be. At least she hoped so.

****

"Are we going to do this every morning?" Paige asked, passing a cardboard carrier of to-go coffee containers to Brooke and Avery whose attention was focused on Arnett and his crew. They scurried around the site amidst the resonating echo of chainsaws and a large chipper they had rented from the hardware store in town. Patterson Milby had been in attendance earlier but disappeared to take a telephone call in his office. Rhem had shown up as if to take Milby's place, leaning against the wall in almost the same spot and looking off towards the yellow LMI vehicles that were looking less like ants off in the distance and more like birds.

"For as long as we can," Rhem answered back, extending his arm for a sip of Avery's coffee.

"Sorry, Rhem, didn't know you'd be here," Paige explained almost hypnotically as she dared not pull her eyes away from the work area.

"Tile guy was super fast last night. He laid the entire first floor outside of the event rooms. I just finished grouting and it's gotta dry before I can seal it." He stole another drink before handing it back to Avery.

"This is surprisingly more exciting than watching paint dry."

"But only slightly," Brooke added. "I don't guess you've any news. Any chance Leopold reached out to the Board instead of me?"

"Nope," Paige nodded. "Not a peep. I doubt Leopold's legal counsel is even on the clock the week of Christmas."

"Not as I recall," Avery added. "I doubt we hear anything till after the first. Arnett said his crew will only work till about noon on Christmas Eve. He thinks they will be in the vicinity of the observation deck in the back the day after Christmas."

Rhem wiped his forearm across his forehead, straining as if he could see beyond where the LMI vehicles were parked on the property that belonged to Ennis Ridgepoint, a local farmer who owned a substantial amount of property in Green River Cove. Over the years, Ridgepoint bought and sold lots of land parcels; property that once sold to a developer was frequently halted upon discovery of Indian artifacts by site workers as the area was being excavated. "Too bad that stretch of land isn't Ridgepoint's. His jinx might buy us a day or two."

Brooke and Paige spun around almost at the exact time, looking in Rhem's direction as if he were a ghost. "That's it!" Paige screamed. "Ridgepoint's jinx!"

"What?" Rhem pushed himself from the wall, his eyes wide with confusion. "What did I say?"

"The Board of Indian Affairs," Brooke exclaimed, slapping her torso and pockets in an attempt to locate her phone.

"I don't understand," Avery was anxious, feeling like an outsider for the first time since returning to Green River Cove.

"Artifacts," Brooke clutched her phone like a lifeline. "The site has not been validated as clear of artifacts. We need the Board of Indian Affairs to appoint surveyors to observe while the ground is being disturbed. If we find anything, the digging has to cease until the site is cleared by the consultant."

"Mr. Hall?" Avery asked, her heart pounding in her chest like a drum.

"Yes," Brooke dialed the phone. "I have his number. Why didn't we think of this sooner?"

For the first time in over a week, they had hope. Hope they could save the bottling company for future generations to enjoy and preserve an important part of Green River Cove history.

Brooke waved a goodbye and disappeared through the plant doors while Mr. Hall's wife searched the garage for her husband. Paige followed a few seconds behind, hoping to gather the Board for an emergency discussion that the sale had not been approved by the Board of Indian Affairs. And to see if that might have any bearing on the sale or the proposed resale.

Rhem and Avery left moments later, holding hands, and practically skipping down the icy road that led to the parking lot. It was a longshot, Avery knew, but it was a shot. And it was more than they'd had just yesterday.

****

Samantha's question was a pertinent one. She was wondering where her mother was going to live after the first of the year. If the plan was to put the North Carolina house up for sale and remain in Green River Cove, how did the fact her grandparents were selling their own home play into her mother's plan?

In all the confusion, her parents' decision to put their own place up for sale had slipped her mind. She had not exactly forgotten. It was more like she had reprioritized it to the back of her pressing issue line. But Samantha was right, with her being only an hour and a half away at college, remaining in Green River Cove was an ideal plan. Samantha could come home as often she wanted, and Avery would be close to her cousin, Gaylin, as well as her friends and extended family. And of course, Rhem, she could not imagine relocating so far away that their relationship could not continue to grow. She lost him once. She did not intend to lose him again.

"Grandma?" Samantha scooted close to her grandmother. "Can I open one of my presents?"

"Just one," she added before Patricia could object. "Mom said you used to let her, Aunt Misty, Uncle Curtis, and Uncle Tim open a gift on Christmas Eve."

"That's two nights away," Patricia explained, but it was evident by the way she looked upon her granddaughter that she was going to concede and let her open a gift. "But I get to pick which one." She wandered around the tree as if she had lost something and was searching among the presents for it. "This one," she handed a tiny box to Samantha and another to Avery. "You can open one too."

"Thank you, Mom," Avery took the box and watched as Samantha opened hers first. The ring was exquisite — tiny to fit Samantha's slender ring finger. It was composed of three tiny stones, a reddish garnet color for January, lavender amethyst for February, and pearl for June. Patricia held up her hand to present her hand where her own ring was on display. Avery pushed her hand towards the others, "It's beautiful. I love it and I will always treasure it."

"This will be our last Christmas in this house," Samantha's throat was tight, her words strained. "I've never been anywhere else but here for Christmas or Thanksgiving," her eyes watered as she wiped at them before any tears could fall.

"We made great memories in this house," Patricia said. "And next year, we'll meet at Misty's or one of the boys, maybe we'll rotate and take turns hosting?"

"But it won't be the same." Samantha's dam broke and the tears fell like rain.

"No baby," Avery pulled her into her arms, "it won't be, but the passage of time never is. There is always something different about each year as it passes." Her thoughts drifted back to the bottling company and how different the community would be if they weren't able to save it. Dozens of people depended on the factory to provide for their families. What would happen to them? There weren't enough open positions in town to support that many families.

"Let's make sure we make this last one count," Avery added, looking across the room to her parents and hoping her words sounded convincing enough because she herself had doubts.

****

"Christmas Eve is tomorrow," Avery blew a cooling breath across her paper cup of coffee. "We're running out of time." She could not get Samantha's tearful proclamation around the family spending their last Christmas at the family home out of her mind. If something did not turn around soon, many other families would be facing the same dilemma.

"And the bulldozer is getting closer," Paige pointed across the yard to where the LMI crew was fast at work, leveling the dirt on the surface where the bulldozer had removed a dozen or so large trees while three of the crew with chainsaws chewed the enormous trees into smaller pieces that could be pushed into the chipper.

Dispersed among the crew, Brendan Hall and three other volunteers walked in and among the ruins, their faces pointed towards the ground as if in prayer.

Maybe they were praying as their eyes focused on the unearthed soil in search of a tool fashioned from a stone or a piece of pottery. Time was running out, they needed to find something that might save the old bottling plant they loved so. They were praying for a miracle and so was the rest of the town.

"What's with those orange flags?" Avery asked, wondering if it was like the electric company and how they marked the ground where the underground electric lines ran.

"If anything turns up on the surface," Brooke explained, "they photograph it exactly as they find it. Using gloves, they carefully remove it for analysis and mark the location with a flag and a number."

"One of the other volunteers logs the items by location and number," Paige went on.

"So, basically we need someone to scream out and hold up one of those flags?" Avery did not realize how sarcastic it came out until she finished asking the question. She would have felt guilty if the commotion nearby did not indicate a potential finding. "They've stopped digging."

"Everyone's moving towards that volunteer with the red shirt on," Paige did not try to curtail the excitement or her disappointment when the work continued and the volunteers returned to their previously assigned areas.

"I'm going to need therapy before this is finished," Avery explained, holding her chest as if she could not get her breath. "I don't know why—"

Across the field, a whistle blew and everyone, including Brendan, moved to the same volunteer in the red shirt. One by one the vehicles slowed, the chainsaws grew silent, and the chipper was turned off. The women watched as the bulldozer came to a halt and Brendan raised an orange flag high in the sky before marking a spot in the ground.

"They have found something," Avery screamed, falling into the arms of Brooke and Paige, and jumping up and down like they had done the night the Dragons won the state tournament by a single basket in double overtime. It was like that only better.

****

The silence of the predawn morning was magical in a way Avery could only imagine it had been years ago on the eve of Christ's birth. The wise men, with their gifts tucked safely away, would have been on the final leg of their journey to lay blessings upon the newborn baby and his parents in a barn where they had fashioned a bed of hay for him to lay.

There must have been times, along the journey, when their faith was tested, shaken perhaps, sometimes. But, they never lost sight of their mission, of the tremendous responsibility they had been given, and the insurmountable importance of the role they would play in changing the fate of the world, forever.

Looking at the line of trucks aligned along both sides of Main Street in preparation for the Silent Night Celebration, she realized a tiny portion of what they must have felt. The task that lay ahead of her felt impossible and her heart was heavy with the ache at the thought of losing it all.

Although, the volunteers were mostly unpacking the vehicles, stacking boxes of supplies and pallets of decorations strategically along the street, most lined up at the single food truck for a cup of coffee to ward off the cold. There was much to be done before sunset and the festival was officially live. She wanted it to be perfect, for her family and friends, and for herself. Afterall, there was a chance it might be their last celebration for a very long time.

"Are you and Rhem okay with being in charge of getting the decorations up?" Paige was at her side, as if she had appeared by magic. It was hard not to laugh, Paige was bundled so snuggly into her thick parka, the string of its hood wrapped like a noose, and fuzzy gloves without finger slots, that made writing on the clipboard in her hand, challenging. The only identifiable portion of her body was her face, and because of the cool predawn air, her eyes were watery, nose red, and the skin of her face, tight across her face.

"Yes," Avery mumbled through chattering teeth. Paige may have looked like the marshmallow man in a red coat, but her attire was definitely a warmer choice than the tweed coat, wool scarf, and leather gloves Avery was wearing. "Is that the diagram for where everything is going? She nodded towards the paper on top of those attached to Paige's clipboard.

"Here's your copy," Paige pushed it into her hand. "No deviations, I know you're the artistic one and all but you're a writer, not a decorator."

"Haven't been a writer in a long time," Avery studied the document and looked past Paige to see if Rhem had arrived yet.

"You are," Paige turned away, her words becoming less audible the further away she walked. "You just need to be reminded."

Right, she thought, moving quickly to take a place in line. Once the sun came up, it would warm up some, but for now, she was freezing. She needed hot coffee, lots of it.

****

"I hope one of those is for me?" Rhem asked as he moved closer to her, eyeing the large cup of coffee in her hand. Once he was close enough, he kissed her cheek and took the cup from her hand, almost in the same action. "Good morning," his lips were warm against her cold cheek.

"I know you're making a fashion statement and all but that is not a proper coat for this type of work. City life done made you crazy." He joked and pulled her into his arms. "Have to start quickly on your reeducation now that you're home. You might freeze to death before Spring."

"Haha," she mocked. "I haven't done anything like this since out Senior year when we volunteered for the Winter fair at school."

"I remember that. I modified Ms. Humphress' sign-up sheet so we could work the snack booth together," he smiled. "She had me doing the basketball booth."

"I didn't know that," she studied him for a moment. "We were still just hanging out together then. You were dating that cheerleader."

"And you were still seeing that football player," he added. "I stopped seeing Susan after the Winter fair. I knew I wanted to me more to you than just your friend."

"And here we are," she fell against him, enjoying the heat that radiated from his body and the warmth of his lips on hers.

"Less kissing, more work, you two," Brooke barked as she approached, but her smile was in contradiction to her directive. Her face said it all. She was pleased, happy they were together.

"Any news?" they pulled apart to face her, anxious for any update.

"No, the area is still roped off where the pieces were uncovered." She stuffed her hands deeper into her pockets, hoping to find a fraction of warmth. "I didn't see any of the pieces they found but Brendan said he thought they were old. Doesn't mean they're Indian artifacts but they are old."

"Anything from Leopold Media?" Avery asked, although she already knew the answer. No one would be in the office this week, probably not next week either. There was very little probability they would hear anything until after the first of the year.

"No, I've emailed a few times, but I haven't gotten anything except out of office messages," Brooke explained. "I'm really not expecting anything back." She motioned across the street to where Paige was waving at her, indicating that she should join her. "I've got to go. The Boss is calling."

"And we better get started on the decorations." She scanned the crowd. "Where are our high school volunteers?"

"Over there by the donuts," Rhem pointed out, pulling her by the arm to where a group of young people dressed in thick, green, school jackets were gathered near the coffee, pushing and pulling at each other in jest.

Off in the distance, only the edge of the night sky was evident as a pink streak of the rising sun poked above the black clouds to announce the coming of the new day. Soon the darkness would give way to the light and as board by board was placed, the Silent Night Celebration began to arise from the pallets and boxes. It was a labor of love, and she was grateful for the opportunity to experience it again, as an adult.

Chapter 11

The magic of Christmas was in the air along with the fragrance of buttery popcorn, sugary fried dough, and meaty ribs smothered in onions and barbeque sauce. There was the scent of cinnamon-topped warm cider and melting whipped-cream-topped hot chocolate hanging on the cusp of cold air, as it hovered like a ghost in and around rows of tables and chairs positioned by a large, flaming bonfire at the end of the street.

On both sides of the street, aligned like a checkerboard on the sidewalk in front of the businesses whose doors had closed for the celebration, vendors selling everything from roasted chestnut to freshly baked muffins and pies huddled together hoping to stay warm. The café and diner were bustling with activity as the outside seating overflowed with patrons gathering at tables stationed close enough to feel the heat that radiated from massive, outside electric heaters. The sound of glass upon glass was prominent as adults toasted one another, offering silent prayers of good will and hope for the upcoming year against a backdrop of holiday music that echoed harmonically into the night as offered by the local high school concert band.

Inside the establishments, customers with outerwear draped over their arms waited, hoping a table might open up soon versus later so they might enjoy a plate of homemade meatloaf and mashed potatoes with thick, greasy gravy.

Farther down the road, past the booth where the Baptist church offered a variety of baked cakes and pies, the choir took their position in front of the live tree and wreath stand, juggling as close as they dared to one of the outside heaters and thumbing through the songbook until coming to the musical arrangement in question. They watched as the conductor took her place, pulling her thick coat close against her body, yet allowing it to remain open as to not restrict the movement of her arms. Monica was a pretty woman, in her mid-thirties with long, curly hair that hung around her shoulders and big, blue eyes only partially visible behind thick, black glasses. She had the voice of an angel and when she opened her mouth in the name of the Lord, there was seldom a dry eye in the sanctuary.

Avery moved as close against him as she could, partly because of the frigid air that kept pushing into the space between them but mostly because of how good it felt to feel the warmth of his body against hers.

She held a warm cup of mulled apple cider as close to Rhem's mouth as she could without tiptoeing on her feet. "You want to finish this?"

"Don't you want it?" he took the thermal cup from her hand, letting his gloved hand linger longer against her than was necessary.

"I'm thinking we can share a big hunk of carrot cake from Paige's booth?" She smiled, "I haven't had it in years, but I bet it's her momma's recipe."

"I was leaning more towards one of the chocolate chip brownies from the church booth?" he finished the last of the cider and tossed the cup in a nearby receptable. "We can get one of each and share!"

"You get the brownie," she kissed his cheek. "I'll get the carrot cake." She weaved in and out of the crowd disappearing as if she were an assailant and was avoiding an arrest. The distance from where she waited with him to Paige's booth was not far at all. It should have simply been a matter of walking the hundred yards or so and waiting her turn in the line. But by the time she stopped to visit with the locals, mostly people she had not seen in many years, Rhem had returned from the church booth and eaten all but a bite or two of the brownie.

"I hope you got another one of those in that bag?" she indicated to the rolled-up paper bag he held in his hand and pushed a paper plate with a slice of carrot cake cut so large, it nearly took up the entire plate.

"After you eat your portion of that cake, I'll get you a brownie if you still want one," he laughed, swooping in close enough to plant a cool kiss upon her lips. She could tell by the way he pulled away, something or someone had caught his eye.

"Arnett?" he offered his hand to LMI's foreman. "Glad you were able to join the celebration."

Avery took a moment to study him, dressed in clean, pressed jeans and denim shirt barely visible beneath a thick, black coat. He had taken the time to shave, his hair combed straight to one side as if he were on his way to church.

"As long as we're hanging around here, waiting on the results of that pottery, figured I should get and savor the flavors of the local municipality." He jammed his hands into his pockets and tipped his weight on the balls of his feet. "Kinda reminds me of where I grew up, back in Indiana."

"Not going to get to go home for the holidays?" Avery asked, her words glazed with sympathy. She had never been away from her parents over the Christmas holiday. Even if her schedule only allowed her a day or two away from work, she had always managed to be home for Christmas Eve and day. She prayed that pattern would continue for her and for her daughter.

"Not this year," Arnett craned his neck awkwardly around the couple, as if being led by the nose and the unearthly smell coming from the barbeque pit where steaks were grilling. "Corporate wants the digging to resume as soon as the area is cleared."

If he saw Avery flinch as if she had been slapped, he gave no indication. Instead, he leaned in closer as if he wanted to share a secret. "I sent most of the crew home till the second of January. Once the site is cleared, it will be a fairly slow pace until the staff is all onsite and working."

"Why are you helping us?" Rhem asked, his hands laying close against his side as if he was in the military and placed at ease.

"Because I know how it feels when the town loses something it loves," he offered. "And if there's even a remote chance your town doesn't have to go through that, I want to help."

"You're a good man, Arnett," Rhem offered his hand again. "And we're grateful."

"We are," Avery added, smiling. "Merry Christmas."

****

It had taken a while but she and Rhem had finally gotten an outside table at Paige's café, close enough to one of the heaters so that they were able to sit comfortably at the table without jackets, hats, and gloves. The wine bottle that rested in the empty space between them was nearly empty and the ceramic platter where remnants of a flat bread pizza remained, left the table seeming smaller than it was. Course, the way they leaned into the center of the table with their hands clasped and their heads close to one another contributed to the small nature of the seating area.

"Can we join you?" Brooke asked, pulling at Avery's satchel so that the empty seat between them could be utilized for something other than her garment storage.

"Please," Rhem stood up, offering Graham a welcoming hand, and waited until Brooke was seated before retaking his seat. He held up the wine bottle, "Wine?"

"Yes," Brooke answered, taking Avery's nearly empty glass and holding it out to be refilled. She waved to the server to bring Graham a clean glass. "Where's our Mayor?"

"Behind the counter," Avery answered, turning to indicate where Paige worked diligently behind the counter to help the servers get the food out to the customers. "She's been by a few times to check on us but hasn't had a chance to actually sit and catch up."

Avery took the glass from Brooke and swallowed several mouthfuls before handing it back to her friend. "Still nothing?"

"I left word with the call center to forward any calls from Brendan to my phone. He promised as soon as he knows anything, he'd call, regardless of the time," Brooke answered, but it was obvious to Avery, there was something else on her mind.

"Did Stephen and his family make it home, yet?" Avery waved to Paige, smiling as Paige untied her apron and made her way towards their table.

"Right before sunset, just in time to accompany us into town," Brooke pointed across the street where her son and his wife watched as their two young sons ran and danced through the artificial snow that fell from the hardware store in town. There had only been a few times in the history of Green River Cove where the town had enjoyed a white Christmas. Luckily, the same could not be said for the children who were fortunate enough to play in the fake snow. It was, as usual, the highlight of the night for the youngsters.

"Your Mom and Dad coming into town for the festival?" Brooke added, in an obvious attempt to distract the conversation away from the fact her youngest son was not going to be in attendance.

"They're enjoying the events from the warmth and comfort of the bookstore," Avery added. "My grandparents are there, too. Dad moved the sofa and chairs towards the store front window so they can see everything."

"Ward has quite the setup, over there," Rhem smiled to Avery. "We should stop by and have a drink with them before the night is over." He pushed his chair closer to Graham so that Paige could push a chair for herself at the table and enjoy the conversation.

"Is Samantha joining us?" Paige asked, dropping a plate of warm muffins into the center of the table. "I saw her with some friends earlier where the band was performing."

"She's here somewhere," Avery answered. "It would be a fate worse than death to be seen socializing with her mother."

"She's over at the bookstore with your parents," Graham added, smiling. "Saw her about fifteen minutes ago." He tossed a muffin on his plate and motioned for Brooke to pass him the saucer fat with a slab of warm butter.

"I want something substantial for dinner," Brooke began, eyeing his muffin with disdain. "You've already had an elephant ear, popcorn, and two caramel apples."

"I've already decided I'm having an extra-large portion of meatloaf with potatoes," he answered, reaching for a second muffin.

"Graham —" Brooke began, jumping as the phone in her pocket screeched and shrilled as if it were alarming. She jumped, running her hands in and out of her coat pockets, before her hand finally wrapped around it. She stole a momentary glance and the caller, smiling when she recognized the number.

"Brendan," she fought to maintain her excitement. "I'm here with Avery and the Mayor, any updates?" She set the phone to speaker and laid it gently atop the table.

"Hi girls," his voice was muffled but easily recognizable as the old mentor they knew and loved from their school days. "I can't tell you how it warms my heart to know the three of you have stayed in one another's lives. When you get to be my age, you'll understand how important relationships are." He cleared his throat, "The fragments we collected from the site are in fact, Apache, probably from the late 1800's early, 1900's."

He paused as the table began to cheer and clap, the girls hugging one another as if they were being reacquainted after many years of being apart. "There may be some challenges with getting the site sanctioned as a protected area, but it will definitely buy us a few more weeks. Plus," he paused, enabling the sound the pages made as his fingers shuffled through them to be more audible. "According to the county doctrine, the sale of the facility will require approval from the Board of Indian Affairs."

Again, there was cheering and clapping, its cadence growing louder as several of the onlookers in the outside seating area, as well as customers on the street, stopped to listen and understood the gravity of the announcement. "Madam Mayor, I assume you've met with Chief Adriel? He'll need to address the Board of Indian Affairs for the approval to continue working the site."

Paige smiled, "he is."

"Can we count on him?" Brendan's question was tinged with excitement. It was easy to imagine him with the phone to his ear and drumming his hands atop the table in rhythm to the up and down motion of his leg against the floor.

"We can," Paige clapped her hands together as if in prayer. "We just need to call an emergency meeting and get on the agenda." She twisted around in her seat to collect her phone from her jacket pocket only to be interrupted by Brooke's cool hand against hers.

"It's Christmas Eve, I'll send an official email to let them know we need to meet first thing Monday morning." Brooke refilled her wine glass and settled comfortably against the back of her chair. "We'll also need to inform Leopold Media of recent events and the impact to both the excavation as well as the ownership change of Cove Bottling."

She held up her glass and moved it towards the center of the table, waiting for the others to collect their glasses and join her in a toast. "Looks like we may have gotten our Christmas miracle, after all." The sound the glasses made as they came together echoed through the room as the patrons at the other tables raised their glasses to celebrate the town's good fortune. It was loud amongst the chatter within the dining area. From the business next door, the artificial snow began to fall again, its flakes carried on the cool wind before covering the short distance to the café and melting upon contact with the patrons as well as the dining tables. The timing of the falling snow was perfect. As if fate had made an appearance and announced to the community of Green River Cove that all was well.

Across the table, Avery caught Rhem's eyes, and smiled as the snowflakes danced between them. The years since high school melted away as effortlessly as the ice particles that dusted his shoulders and those that melted once engaged with the warm strands of his hair. There was only her and him and the holiday music that echoed from the end of the street as the church choir entertained onlookers with this year's Christmas cantata.

"Mama," a male voice called from the other side of the street, as the table turned to determine the caller's identity. It was obvious he was a soldier, his army green jacket and black wool cap a dead giveaway. "Mama," he called out again, once he was closer, his arms stretched out to Brooke.

"Patrick," Brooke cried, nearly falling over her feet to get to him. It was as if she feared he might be an apparition and would disappear before she could hold him, look upon him with her own eyes. She fell into his arms, not realizing her thick winter jacket and gloves were draped over the restaurant chair.

"Patrick," her tears ran down her face like rain while her hands flapped against his chest and cheek as if to validate to her brain that he was there in the flesh with her. "I thought you weren't going to get leave?"

Graham joined them in the street, patting his son's shoulder before falling into the embrace with Brooke and Patrick. "Welcome home, son."

"My commander asked if anyone could be ready to leave in 8 minutes or less for a single seat headed home." Patrick smiled, his face more closely resembling his father's than his mother's. Patrick was the spitting image of his father — whereas his brother, Stephen, looked like a masculine version of his mother. What a heartwarming picture they made, mother, father, and sons — an image that would be imprinted upon the community's heart for years to come.

"Let's go home," Brooke took her son's hand with one hand and pulled her husband with the other. Miracles were in the air tonight and she could not wait to get home, where Stephen and his family were waiting, so that she could give thanks for her life's many blessings and celebrate that her entire family was together.

Avery watched as Brooke made her way down the street to where she and Graham had parked their vehicle. It took only a minute or two before the car pulled away and headed towards the old Donansburg Road. Avery's heart was happy, full to the extreme, in knowing that her friend's Christmas wish had come true. And a few of her own had as well.

"Cousin!" Gaylin ran up to the table as if she were being pursued before coming to a halt next to Rhem and Avery's table. "If you want some help packing up the North Carolina house after the holidays, let me know."

"I might have to take you up on that," Avery took her cousin's hand. "Think you can borrow one of Ms.

Lorene's trucks from the flower shop? Might need some help with some of my smaller, more delicate things I wouldn't want the movers to take."

"I'm sure I can," she smiled. "Might need to practice a bit backing in and out, though." She checked her watch, "I got to go, Richard's over at Uncle Ward's. Too cold for him out here. Merry Christmas, Cousin. It's so good to have you home."

"Merry Christmas to you, too. I'll see you tomorrow at Mom's for dinner?"

"We'll be there," her cousin waved as her figure retreated towards the bookstore.

"Does that mean you're staying here in Green River Cove?" Rhem's words across the table were hypnotic, his eyes magnets to hers. "Not everyone gets a second chance." He held his hand out to hers. "We can build an amazing life here together, if you will allow it."

"I am," she answered, not breaking contact with his eyes. "My parents are looking to sell their house. I'm in the market for a place to live. Will be a win-win for both of us."

It was a perfect solution—one she could not take credit for. It was Samantha's suggestion, last night as she was getting ready for bed. Her nightly visits to her mother's room were not uncommon to share and unwind from the day's events and place a quick kiss upon her mother's cheek. Within three minutes of falling into the bed and crawling on her knees to rest her back against the headboard, she proposed the transaction between her mother and grandparents.

The best of both worlds, she had said as part of her closing argument. The only place the family had ever celebrated Christmas in, would remain in the family, her grandparents could plan the retirement trip of their dreams, and her mother's new life in Green River Cove could begin as soon as the North Carolina house sold for a respectful profit.

There was no need for Avery to take any additional time to consider Samantha's plan. She was correct. It made the most sense, buying her parents' home was the right thing to do. Everyone would get what they wanted, including a new start for Avery and Rhem.

"Finish your wine," he emptied his glass and pulled her to her feet. "I want to show you something."

"But the cantata isn't over, yet. I love the holiday music," but she stood and gathered her outerwear, just the same.

"We aren't going far," he slid her jacket over her arms, pausing long enough to plant a warm kiss against her cheek. "Just over to the hotel, we can listen to the music as we walk, and I'll open and prop the door open once we get there."

"What is it?" her interest was piqued. She loved a good surprise, especially a Christmas one.

"You'll see," he led her from the café and took her hand. The walk took only a minute or two, even counting the time it took for him to fumble in his pocket for the key. The room was cool once they were inside, nothing a healthy fire in the hearth could not have remedied.

Instead, he propped open one of the two double doors and walked deeper into the hotel, flipping lights as he went so that the room was lit in an eerie glow that radiated yellow across the room.

She considered shifting out of her coat but opted to keep it on instead. Even with the coat on, she was trembling underneath, and she was not sure it was entirely a result of the weather. "You've gotten a lot accomplished," she wandered closer to the check-in desk and ran her gloved hand over its rich surface. He had polished the dark wood so that the grain stood out in deep contrast to the lighter color of the surface. "It's beautiful."

"Yes," he whispered, catching her profile in the lamplight, "it is but that's not what I want to show you." He stopped near the door that led into the small room, the one he thought may have been a telephone room years earlier. "What do you think of this?"

She moved to where he indicated, her heart pounding at the thought of what he could have done that would have mattered to her. The hotel was his and his personality was alive everywhere she looked. It was in the floral wallpaper over the desk and the fabric of the sofa and loveseat. It was in the furniture that occupied the lobby and the red velvet drapes that gathered in a pile upon the floor. He had breathed his life into the place as surely as if it were a living, breathing appendage of himself.

Her breath caught in her throat as she looked deeper into the room. He had fashioned the tiny room with a dainty wooden desk and chair, side table with an ornamental 1800's reproduction lamp with a chain pull-string to switch the lamp on and off. Built into the wall to the immediate right of the desk was an elaborate bookcase, filled with books with classic leather covers. The bottom shelf was filled with copies of Avery's best-selling novel as well as a single copy of her collection of short stories. Somehow, Rhem had acquired the final copy, the last of the four she had printed from the publisher. She knew there were four copies and three were in the possession of her parents at the store. How he had sequestered it was a mystery and she did not care. The fact was, he had the book, he had held onto it after all the years as if he knew fate would bring them together again.

"You turned it into a writing room?" her words were above a whisper.

"I did," he moved closer. "You can start writing again—"

She cut him off, "That was a lifetime ago, Rhem. I'm not even sure I have anything to say, anything to share anymore."

"You'll find your words again or they'll find you," his arms wrapped around her waist as he pulled her as close as he could. "I love you and I want to spend the rest of my life listening to your stories."

"I love you too." She moved into his kiss. It was perfect, like all the holidays collided together and came to reside in the warmth of his lips. It was as if they had never been apart, as if she had never gone away. She was home, and with God's grace, there would never be a need to be anywhere else.

Chapter 12

Matthew's Leopold's reaction to the news of the site's shutdown should have been better predicted. He was not a patient man and not used to his directives not being followed to the letter of his law. It was frustrating enough that the project was not on schedule, Arnett had piddled around at the site, until the locals had been successful in uncovering a valid reason to halt the project.

The lawyer for Green River Cove had wasted no time in seeking an injunction for the excavation to cease. That was how it was in small towns, everyone knew everyone. Seeking and granting favors were simply par for the course. His directive to Arnett should have been specific, start with the building and level it to the ground. Instead, Matthew had left it to chance and now the entire deal was off. The initial sale had been voided by the State, pending approval from the Director of the Indian Affairs. That approval could take years and the amount of company resources that would be tied up waiting for consent would impede the company's growth and ability to support new developments. It would be easier and less expensive to destroy the agreement and allow Patterson Milby to return the money. It would be as if the purchase had never happened. Sometimes, he wished he had never heard of Cove Bottling or Rush soda.

****

Patterson Milby dressed in denim jeans and a black turtleneck sweater looked out of place in the conference room at Green River Cove Bottling, which was an oddity since he had spent over half his life residing or participating in discussions within the room. In the eight days since Brooke forwarded to him the full executed agreement, bill of sale, and cashier's check, he had never experienced a myriad of such emotions. Beginning with satisfaction and a sense of excitement for the many doors the acquisition by Leopold Media had opened. His high hopes had fallen, like a rock, once presented with the new direction the company would be taking with the project. Nothing had worked out the way it was supposed to, it was as if the deal was jinxed.

Perhaps, once the money for the sale was returned to Matthew Leopold, the chain of misfortune might break and put things right again. Ownership of Cove Bottling, by governing law, was once again in his and his family's hands. And as the passage of time reverted to the way it was, so would the struggle to keep the business afloat. By his own calculation, there was little more than six months of available funds to pay for supplies and operational expenses. Was bankruptcy a better plan for Cove Bottling than what Matthew Leopold had planned?

He made his way anxiously to his feet and turned to the door upon hearing the sound of Avery, Brooke, and Paige's footsteps upon the old hardwood floors of the front entrance near all the way through the main corridor of the executive offices and conference areas. Given the beginning of the New Year was less than a week away, new production lines were shut down. Only the distribution lines and drivers were working the short week leading to the holiday. Historically, keeping the shelves full of Rush soda for holiday parties had yielded good returns in exchange for the overtime to drivers paid out during the week. More importantly, was ensuring the community had access to its most favorite hometown drink.

"Hope you all had a good Christmas." he motioned toward the empty chairs around the table, inviting them to take a seat.

"We did. It was a miracle Patrick made it home to us for the holiday." Brooke spoke first, flopping her satchel atop the table as if it were her lunch in a brown, paper bag. "And now that Leopold Media's legal team has returned the addendum to the initial agreement indicating that agreement is null and void, we realize that the challenges that prompted you to seek out their partnership in the first place, still exists."

Patterson did not respond, but simply nodded his head and framed his hand over his mouth and chin as if he had more to say but wanted to ensure the words could not escape from his mouth. He was a good-looking man, even at his age, his hair was mostly blonde. In school, he had worn his hair longer, layered along the sides, and parted in the middle so that there was nothing for his big, blue eyes to hide behind. He had an infectious smile, all of his brothers did, but his was always the most pronounced.

"We have no more than six, maybe seven months of reserve in the company bank account. I will have to approach the Board of Directors about securing a loan sometime in the Summer, if we continue with our existing business plan."

"About that," Avery chimed. "I realize you might feel a bit burned over our recent endeavor with Leopold Media, but have you considered a partner more local, one who understands the role Cove Bottling plays in our community's history?"

"I've approached Michael Cox in Campbellsville and Everett Durham over at the stockyard. Neither had an interest." He sighed and ran his hand over his head. "I fear we have simply postponed the inevitable."

"Maybe not," Paige moved to the coffee bar and poured three cups of coffee before returning to the conference table and taking her seat. "We have a proposition for you to consider."

Patterson's posture straightened, his back rigid against the seat as the one leg crossed over the other moved so that both his feet were on the floor. "You've got my attention."

"I have a potential client who recently came into a large sum of money and has some interest in investing a portion in Cove Bottling." Brooke smiled, her eyes lit up, her iris' seemingly more white than blue. "One who won't have any interest in making drastic changes to the plant or its operations."

"I do want to make changes to the operations," Avery blurted out as if she were seven years old and selected a puppy from the shelter. "Just not ones that are in contradiction to the history of the plant."

"You want to invest?" Patterson asked, his words lagging behind his brain as he fought to process what Brooke had said about an investor. It was common knowledge Avery had resigned from Leopold Media, rather than return to work there after the holidays. He assumed she had some sort of contractual severance package but had no idea the amount was extreme enough to consider becoming a partner in Cove Bottling.

"I do," she smiled, placing her arms atop the table as if it were a bench and she was the judge. "But I'll be more silent than Leopold. The strategy we presented to you, months ago, was mostly mine. I want to implement some of those efficiencies to the plant and expand the distribution routes into other regions outside Green River Cove." She looked to her friends for support and went on. "We'll proceed slowly and make the changes at your pace."

"What amount are you looking to invest?" Patterson opened his hands out in front them, minimizing the distance between.

Brooke pushed a stapled agreement towards him and leaned back to await his perusal. "It's all spelled out in the agreement. She'll make the investment in installments and has the option to make changes based on the market and how the new distribution routes are received by Franklin and Pulaski counties."

"There are 120 counties in the bluegrass state," Paige added. "Only three states in America have more. We plan to have Cove Soda available in all 120 counties over the next five years."

"What about the expansion Leopold Media said we needed before we could expand beyond our existing service area?" He bit his tongue. "We've opened up a can of worms that can't be sealed now that Adriel's involved. The Indian Affairs Office's approval to proceed will still be needed to renovate the dock."

"We won't need to expand beyond the perimeter of the existing dock," Avery added, "We'll use more resistant material that can easily be converted into transitional bays and can be used for both incoming and outgoing parcels."

"And if space becomes an issue," Brooke added, "we build up not out."

Patterson took a moment to study the drawings included with the agreement. "And you'll draw a modest salary with dividends paid out annually?" Patterson thumbed through the rest of the document. "I'll have to have Davis take a look since you're representing the other party," he smiled. "But I think it will be fine." He offered his hand. "Thank you for this, I hope this venture is mutually beneficial for us all."

"I think it will be," Avery smiled. "And I'm quite pleased that this journey has brought me home again. I feel as if I've been given a second chance and I have every intention of getting it right this time. She smiled and watched as Patterson collected the document and disappeared through the threshold of the conference door.

"Quite a turn of events," Paige waited until Patterson closed the door behind him. "New job, new home, and rekindled romance for an old flame. Sounds like the making of a Hallmark movie."

"It does," Avery smiled, knowing she could not agree more. All that was missing was a wide- angle view of Green River Cove's Main Street barely visible through the white, fat, falling snow. Christmas lights of every color would be barely visible as snow flurries clung to the windows, making the houses look almost magical, like edible gingerbread. There would be jovial, holiday music that would decrescendo as the screen gently faded to black. All would be well, and everyone would live happily ever after, content in the knowledge that Christmas miracles do exist, and second chances are born again in the hearts of those who truly believe that, with love, all things are possible.

Extras

Holiday Short Story
Christmas Cards from Heaven

I wasn't really sure what to expect as I sat down to go through my mom's Christmas boxes. To say I had spent the last six months dreading it would be an understatement. The boxes and bins had been stacked delicately in my garage since they had arrived from what had been the home she shared with my father for nearly thirty-five years.

Since the moment my mom passed away in April, my heart has missed her every minute of every hour. There is a void; a loneliness I know will never be resolved. Parts of my life are empty now with huge pieces that stab at my heart. The ache is continuous, but there are times I am smothered by the thought of her, the realization that I can't call her on the phone or drive over. It is at its worst around the holidays, especially Christmas.

My mom loved Christmas; her tree perfect, centered dominantly in the small confines of the living room. Painstakingly she would hang lights and garland around the mirror and entertainment center, warming every space with the prospect of Christmas cheer. Her animated dolls and centerpieces were strategically visible from the entryway as if their mission was to awe and inspire from the minute you walked through the door. Although it was different after my father passed away, she still made every visit feel like coming home, especially around the holidays.

That sense of breathlessness never left me. Years later, after I had moved out and made a family of my own, it was still there intermingled with the soft sweet smells of carrot cake and turkey every time I crossed the threshold into her house.

Years earlier Mom had begun decorating in July, with a plan to be finished with her house by the end of October. Every year, a few days before Halloween, she would arrive at my house, drag the bins from the attic and begin making the inside of my home look like Santa's workshop. The first years, she worked on only the common areas, family room, living room, etc. But it seemed with each passing year, she added another room, kitchen, kid's room, and master bedroom. Ultimately, every room had a theme and was decorated accordingly, from snowmen in the bathrooms to the poinsettia garland draping the bookshelves in the study. Christmas was alive and present in every corner of my house. And it was just as magical as when I was a child.

Her house is empty now. The walls are bare, each and every room, awaiting new stories to play out with a new family. The opening of the front door echoed loudly through the house as I pushed it with enough force to disengage the realtor lock box. Thanksgiving, I thought to myself. Her tree would be up. My mind's eye saw decorations placed exactly where they belonged, twinkling in synchrony against a holiday soundtrack of Amy Grant. The tree, perfection in every string of lights, garland, and ornaments materialized against the wall, its skirt not visible under the brightly colored stacked packages of gifts.

My steps resonated loudly as I made my way into the kitchen. It wasn't hard to imagine the smell of sugary desserts she would no doubt be in the middle of preparing. Her image was so clear I had to pause and reconsider, accept she was not there, and move further into the house. It had not taken much time at all to walk through and remember the thirty-five Christmas' past. I smiled at the thought of Dad on the roof with Christmas lights in hand and my brother trading candy items from Dad's stocking when Mom wasn't looking. I felt it all again, tasted the collard green soup on Christmas Eve and Grandma's three-layer carrot cake. It was as if time had stopped and regifted the memories to me. My mom, my dad, and brother—the family of this house—aren't here anymore. There won't be dinner or presents to open on Christmas morning. The ache was overwhelming, and I dropped to my knees for support. Minutes later, I wiped away the tears and pulled myself up from the floor, comforted by the thought that they are together again this Christmas in Heaven.

Finding the unused Christmas cards buried in the box, really wasn't a surprise. I knew she bought them every year after the holiday for the next year. They were beautiful. Some with country snow covered barns and old red pick-up trucks adorned with holiday decorations; others with majestic Christmas trees, highlighted in gold and silver glitter. The red birds caught my eye, coupled together sitting atop a snow-covered tree branch.

I looked guiltily around my living room, there wasn't a Christmas decoration in sight, and it was nearly Thanksgiving. Normally, Mom and I would be finishing up my house in preparation for her return to her own home. I had not really considered the decorations, any of them, mine or hers, after my brother, Curtis', funeral in September. The thought of the traditions of our past that previously had brought so much joy, were suffocating me. My goal since Halloween had pretty much been to just get through the holidays in one piece, physically and emotionally.

As I sat there remembering chili dinners on the first cool night of Fall and opening thirty years of Holiday Barbies, I realized that is not what my family was about. Holidays were such a big part of who we were, who I am, it felt wrong not to honor them and ensure the traditions continued for my daughter and the family she would have one day. The message was as clear as if Mom were sitting with me, stringing new lights or arranging worn wreath bows. The spirit of Christmas lives on, long after each of us draws our last breath. It's in the old two-dimensional Rudolph television show and in Granny's poinsettia china with the nicked edge. You can see traces of Christmas past on the silver angel tree topper and worn red tree skirt that belonged to Grandma. It was as if a time capsule was opened, I remembered so many long-forgotten recollections.

Quickly, I gathered all of the cards and matched them to their envelopes, scribbling into each one as if I were being timed. Letter by letter, I combed through my address book, hoping there would be enough to distribute to my aunts, uncles, and cousins, as well as the people important in their lives.

I blew a sigh of relief as I finished addressing the cards, delighted to discover there was only one red bird card left. With tears building, I signed the card and dropped it into the ceramic Santa card holder Mom made when I was nine years old.

Merry Christmas from Heaven, Mom, Dad, & Curtis.

The End

About the Author

Lisa Robin Phillips Colodny was born and grew up in the rural countryside of Kentucky. She attended the University of Kentucky and Broward College in Fort Lauderdale and graduated with a Doctorate in Pharmacy from Nova Southeastern University.

Her non-fiction publishing history includes numerous publications in the health and science industry. Other titles currently available by this author include an award-winning children's book, Ms. *Abrams' Everything Garden*, and adult fiction, *The Town Time Forgot,* and *Yellow River Pledge*.

Lisa Colodny

Dr. Colodny currently works in the healthcare industry and resides in South Florida with her daughter and their Labrador retriever, Cooper.

Also by the Author

The Town Time Forgot Series
Turbulence
Crossroads
Terminus
Yesterday, Once More

A Rescue Me Series Novel
Chimera

The Coven Queens Series
Wavering Moon

Journeys
Sanctuary Road
Sultana
Yellow River Pledge
As Written

The Place Where Magic Lives
Into the Woods
Walking the Plank
Promise of Wishing Rock

Illustrated Children's Novels
Ms. Abrams' Everything Garden
Jericho Alley

Lisa Colodny

Christmas at Green River Cove

About the Publisher

Kingston Publishing Company, founded by C.K. Green, is dedicated to providing authors an affordable way to turn their dream into a reality. We publish over 100+ titles annually in multiple formats including print and ebook across all major platforms.

We offer every service you will ever need to take an idea and publish a story. We are here to help authors make it in the industry. We want to provide a positive experience that will keep you coming back to us. Whether you want a traditional publisher who offers all the amenities a publishing company should or an author who prefers to self-publish, but needs additional help – we are here for you.

Now Accepting Manuscripts!
Please send query letter and manuscript to:
submissions@kingstonpublishing.com

Visit our website at www.kingstonpublishing.com

CPSIA information can be obtained
at www.ICGtesting.com
Printed in the USA
LVHW081700130123
737018LV00008B/386

9 781645 334019